the
Collected

the Collected

K. R. Alexander

Scholastic Inc.

All rights reserved. Published by Scholastic Inc., *Publishers since 1920*. SCHOLASTIC and associated logos are trademarks and/or registered trademarks of Scholastic Inc.

The publisher does not have any control over and does not assume any responsibility for author or third-party websites or their content.

ISBN 978-1-338-62070-2

10 9 8 7 6 5 4 3 2 1   20 21 22 23 24

Printed in the U.S.A.   40
First printing 2020

Book design by Baily Crawford

To the countless readers
who begged for more:
This book is for—and
because of—you.

I've always had a strange fascination with dolls.

For as long as I could remember, they'd been my favorite toys. I never knew why. It's not that I especially enjoyed dressing them up, or even playing make-believe. It's more like . . . dolls always seemed like friends. Better friends than real people, or better than my big sister, Josie, at least.

Dolls were always there for me.

To listen.

To help.

To share.

Maybe that's why I liked them so much.

At night, I could hear them talking. Could hear them whispering secrets that made me feel a little less alone. A little less strange. The only person who made me feel that way was my grandma Jeannie . . . until she was gone.

Dolls don't die on you when you need them most. Dolls don't abandon you. Dolls live forever. They are the perfect family. The perfect friends.

I've always had a strange fascination with dolls. But I suppose that's not all.

Dolls have also had a strange fascination with *me*.

If only I'd known that fascination would turn deadly . . .

1

One of my first memories is of my doll putting her hands around my throat.

I was four. Maybe five.

I was in my bedroom, playing with my toys— a stuffed bear, a stuffed bird, and a princess doll. Princess Honeysuckle was my favorite. We went on the most exciting adventures together. Sometimes we flew to the moon and ruled over aliens. Other times we cast magical spells over our enemies. This time, I think, we were playing house. It's hard to remember.

I just remember that one moment, I was lying on the ground, playing with Mr. Bear and Ms. Parrot.

I looked over and saw that Princess Honeysuckle wasn't on her throne, ruling over her kingdom.

It wasn't the first time she'd gone missing like that.

But it *was* the first time it happened in the middle of playtime.

Normally, she just vanished when I went to bed, and I would blame my sister for coming in and stealing my toys while I was asleep. Not that Josie ever admitted what she'd done. The dolls would always show up after I yelled at her, though. In a day or two.

I was about to call out to Josie—maybe she'd snuck in while I wasn't paying attention.

And that's when I felt it.

Two tiny hands on my neck.

Wrapping around my throat from behind.

I yelled and sat up, tossing my stuffed animals to the side as I grabbed for whatever was squeezing me.

I found Princess Honeysuckle smiling at me.

Her lips and eyes were tinged with red.

Her arms were open as wide as my neck.

Maybe it was my imagination, but I remember her head twisting around—all the way around—and a giggle coming from somewhere deep inside her plastic body.

Then my mom came in. She had heard me scream.

"Are you okay, Anna?" she asked.

"The doll," I said. "She . . . she . . ."

Except when I looked at Princess Honeysuckle again, she looked perfectly normal—plastic smile, dazed eyes, arms serenely at her sides.

Mom took the doll. I never saw it again.

2

It didn't take long to sense that something was wrong with me.

Princess Honeysuckle was the first doll I remember playing with, but she wasn't the last. Nor was she the last to go . . . strange.

When I was in first grade, I remember playing with other girls at recess. It was winter. After the holidays. We'd had show-and-tell that morning, and everyone brought in their new toys. Most of the girls had gotten new dolls, and we sat playing together in our corner of the gym while a blizzard stormed outside.

Even in first grade, I didn't really have friends. I

remember being so excited, because dolls were the one thing I felt comfortable around. Maybe dolls would help me make new friends.

I couldn't have been more wrong.

My new doll, Adventurer Aurora, was the coolest doll I'd ever had. She came with all sorts of neat gadgets—binoculars and a Jeep and a working compass. Even Josie was jealous of her. Back then, Josie and I were still friends. Back then, she still treated me like her sister.

Adventurer Aurora was investigating a forgotten tomb with my new friend's doll, Mountaineer Mary, when Justina—the girl I was playing with—got up to go to the bathroom. I carried on playing without her. The dolls crept deeper into the shoebox caves, avoiding acid bats and fire mummies. And when Justina came back, she yelped out in fear.

"What are you doing?" she asked.

I was confused. "Playing," I told her.

She grabbed Mountaineer Mary and kicked over the shoebox cave, leaving Adventurer Aurora to climb out from the rubble. Justina ran over to the rest of the girls and started whispering. I remember them looking at me strangely. I just dipped my head and went back to playing with Aurora.

As the weeks passed and I watched how my friends played with their dolls, I realized why Justina had been so freaked out. It wasn't my fault, though. Really.

How was I supposed to know that dolls were only supposed to move if you were moving them?

How was I supposed to know that dolls shouldn't be able to walk or crawl or adventure on their own?

I thought that was how everyone played with dolls.

I didn't realize that to everyone else, dolls were just pieces of inanimate plastic.

When *I* played with my dolls, they played back.

3

When I was seven, we went to visit my grandmother and ended up staying for almost a year.

I didn't remember much about that time. I'd spent so many nights trying to remember what happened, but it's like a part of me blocked it out, and Josie refused to talk about it. Like she was scared.

But why would she be scared of the time we spent at Grandma Jeannie's? Grandma was a sweet old woman who lived in a big house by the woods—I remembered that much. Just like I remembered she had a lot of rules to live by. Maybe that's why Josie didn't like talking about it. She hated rules.

I didn't remember much about the school in that town, though I did remember not really having friends except for one. I just couldn't remember her name.

I also didn't remember what we did all year, though sometimes I woke up in the dead of night yelling. Something told me it had to do with our stay at Grandma Jeannie's . . . but it didn't tell me why.

The one thing I *could* remember was Grandma Jeannie.

When I was with her, everything seemed to be okay. We'd moved there because Mom had lost her job and Grandma was getting old and losing her memory. Being around Grandma when she couldn't remember who we were was always really hard. But when she was her old self, she was my friend. We could talk about anything and everything.

Except for dolls.

That was the one rule of Grandma Jeannie's I could remember, maybe because it didn't make any sense to me.

No dolls in the house.

It was hard to be angry with her about it, though. I didn't need dolls with her around. She was my best friend. My only friend. That was about the time Josie started treating me like I was a stranger, one she didn't want to hang around. It hurt my feelings, because we used to be close. I even remember sleeping in her room a couple times when I was scared. Scared of . . . something waiting in the woods outside my window.

When Josie was too distant or Mom was too busy, Grandma Jeannie was there to take care of me. To make sure I was okay and happy and heard. I knew living there wasn't perfect, but when Grandma Jeannie was her old self, my friendship with her was. When my mom got a new job in the city and it was clear Grandma Jeannie could be on her own again, we left. It was one of the worst days of my life.

I'll never forget waving to Grandma as she watched us from the front porch with tears in her eyes.

I just wished I could remember why a place that felt more like home than Chicago ever did could still give me nightmares.

4

After we left, Josie vowed she would never set foot in Grandma's house again.

We were back in Chicago, in our new, slightly bigger apartment. I was in my room, playing with the dolls I hadn't seen in nearly a year, using their storage boxes as mansions and mountains. Mom was out getting groceries when Josie passed by my room. She must have seen me playing through the cracked door.

Immediately, she stormed in and grabbed the dolls from my hands.

"Never," she growled. "You are never playing with

these again. I can't believe, after everything we went through. After everything that happened to you . . ."

"What . . . what happened?" I asked. Because I couldn't remember, and I knew I *should* remember, and this was as close to admitting what happened as Josie had ever gotten.

She breathed heavily, clearly angry. I almost thought she was going to throw the dolls at me—I'd never seen her this mad before.

Instead, she chucked the dolls into a storage box.

"Hey!" I yelled. I tried to stop her, but she was bigger than me. I grabbed her arm as she picked up more dolls and threw them into the box.

She yelped. Jumped back.

She shook out her hand as if I had shocked her. For a brief moment, the skin where I had grabbed her looked different. Like porcelain. Then it faded, though her anger didn't.

She gathered up the rest of my dolls and threw them all into the box, hefting it up and glaring at me.

"This is all Grandma Jeannie's fault," she said. "We are never going back there. Never!"

Then she turned and stormed down the hall.

I heard the door open and slam. I wanted to run after her, to stop her, but the shock of what happened rooted me to the spot. When she came back in, the box was nowhere to be seen. She'd thrown my dolls in the dumpster outside. No matter how hard I cried that night, no matter how much I wished they would come back, I knew I'd never see them again.

Without Grandma Jeannie or my dolls, I felt terribly alone.

And from there, it only got worse.

5

On my ninth birthday, Mom got me a doll. I was so ecstatic when I opened the package—a new Astronaut Amy doll, just what I'd always wanted.

Mom smiled at my happiness.

Josie flipped out.

She grabbed the doll and started yelling. Saying that she wasn't going to stay here if there were dolls in the house. That our apartment needed to become a doll-free zone.

She threw out Astronaut Amy before I even got a chance to unwrap her.

Mom was clearly upset. She scolded Josie, but she

didn't ground my sister. In fact, she took Josie's side. *That* hurt my feelings more than anything else.

Later that night, while I was crying myself to sleep over what was easily the worst birthday ever—the only good thing was the card from Grandma Jeannie, where she said I could come back and stay whenever I wanted—Mom came in and sat down on my bed. She tried to soothe me for a little bit.

"Here," she said, and handed me a wrapped present.

I thought maybe it was Astronaut Amy, but it was some board game I knew I'd never play. I wanted to throw it in the trash. Before I could ask Mom why she had let Josie throw away my toys, she ruined any hope I had of having a real conversation.

"It's clear dolls upset your sister," she said. "So I think it's best if we just give her this one. Okay? No dolls in the house. It will be just like at your grandma's."

Except there, I had Grandma Jeannie to talk to. Here, I don't have anyone.

I didn't say that, though. I didn't say anything. I knew in that moment that Mom had taken Josie's side, and Josie didn't want me to have dolls or friends or to be happy.

Mom kissed me goodnight and left.

Later, as I was falling asleep, I swore I heard Josie pause outside my door. I swore I heard her whisper, *It's for your own good.*

That night, I dreamed of a cabin in the woods. Cackling laughter. A shadowy monster with glowing white eyes. And dolls. Hundreds and hundreds of dolls.

The next day, when I woke up, Astronaut Amy was sitting on my counter. Staring at me.

I didn't take any chances. With tears in my eyes, I threw her in the trash outside before Josie could find her.

"I'm sorry," I whispered as I closed the bin lid. "But you have to stay here."

It felt like burying my last friend.

Grandma Jeannie was the only person who seemed to see me . . . when she was able to see me. It seemed like her memory was getting worse and worse. Sometimes, she and I would talk for hours. Other times, we would go the whole weekend without her knowing who Mom or I were.

Josie never came with us. I thought it was horribly rude, especially after Grandma became sick, but Josie always had a reason to stay home. An excuse. Things to study for, soccer games, even homework. After that yearlong visit, I don't think Josie ever saw Grandma Jeannie again, save for the one time we brought Grandma Jeannie to Chicago for the holidays.

That time didn't count either, because Grandma Jeannie spent those few days believing she was seventeen again and kept thinking that my mom was her mom. Josie tried to laugh it off, but I knew she was sad. I heard her crying in her room when Mom took Grandma Jeannie back home.

But the times when it was just Grandma Jeannie and me, when she was fully aware of who she was and where we were . . . those were some of the best times of my life. Sitting on the porch drinking sun tea, talking about life and school. She always told me that it was okay that I didn't have friends right now. I was different from everyone else. Like she was. That made us unique. Special.

She thought I was special.

Josie just thought I was weird.

Sometimes, Grandma Jeannie would tell me other things. Things that made more sense than they should have. She said that people like her and me saw the world differently. We saw the life force in all things. That was why sometimes it felt like I wasn't alone in an empty room, or why it often felt like I was being watched. She said that I had to be patient with Josie, because she didn't see things the same way I did. We each had our own talents, our own things that made us special. But mine, Grandma said . . . mine set me apart.

I'd tell her about all the strange things that happened to me—like when I'd wake up in the middle of the night hearing whispers, or when I saw things that weren't there from the corner of my eye—and she listened and understood and didn't judge.

The one thing I never told her about was the dolls. Not after the first time I'd mentioned them to her; she got so upset she started yelling, saying I must avoid them at all costs, because they were "her tools." I didn't know who she was talking about, but she kept looking to the woods behind her house when she said it. Scared.

So the dolls remained my secret. How they spoke to me. How they moved around me. How, sometimes, I felt more like a doll than a human kid, or the dolls felt more human than anyone in school. Like Grandma Jeannie, the dolls had always seemed to understand me.

Until Josie made sure to take them away.

7

Back home, I felt I was walking through a different world. Nobody saw things the way I saw them. Especially Josie.

Ever since our time living with Grandma Jeannie, the things that made me feel different only grew stronger. And harder to keep secret. I did my best to keep them from Josie and Mom. I even kept them secret from Grandma Jeannie. Because it wasn't the whispers in the night or the sensation that I could feel more than most people.

It was the dolls.

Even though I wasn't allowed dolls in the house, I still encountered them.

The worst was the sleepover.

It had been a really strange morning. I'd woken up from more nightmares. Nightmares of being trapped in a cabin filled with tiny porcelain dolls, all of them with their eyes crossed out with marker. Nightmares of a giant shadow in the corner. Getting bigger. Growing closer. Devouring the dolls one by one, until its tendrils wrapped around me and swallowed all the light, laughing maniacally.

Maybe that was why I felt off when I met up with my friends.

Alicia and Soo-ji were the only girls who were willing to hang out with me, and it took all my concentration not to act strangely around them. We were walking down the streets of Chicago, and Alicia said we should run to the toy store to pick up toys and games for our sleepover that night. My gut dropped at the thought. Toy stores meant only one thing: dolls.

But I agreed, because like I said, I didn't want

them to think I was weird, and what kid *doesn't* want to go to a toy store?

It started innocently enough. We walked to the board game section first and after a few minutes had picked out a couple games to play that night. I could have sighed with relief as we headed back to the register.

Until we walked past the doll section.

It felt like my stomach dropped to my feet.

I dragged my feet the entire way through the doll aisle. With every step, I felt . . . something . . . within me building. A static. A buzz that filled my ears and made my fingers tingle. I tried to focus on everything except the countless dolls staring at me, their eyes burning the back of my neck. I could feel them. Hundreds of them. Staring at me from behind their plastic screens. The tingle within me grew.

I could hear them. All of them. Whispering to me. Calling my name. Some of them young, childlike. But one was old and creepy, raspy like the wind around gravestones.

Anna. Annaaaaaa.

"Anna!" Alicia called. "Earth to Anna. Hurry up!"

I jolted and looked up.

At that moment, the buzzing inside me snapped. So, too, did the head of every doll in the aisle. All of them snapping to attention, staring straight at me. Alicia didn't seem to notice—she and Soo-ji were at the end of the aisle, watching me impatiently.

I didn't walk the rest of the way to them.

I ran.

8

I try not to think about the sleepover.

I try not to think about what happened.

Mostly because, when I called Mom to pick me up from Alicia's house, after the disastrous attempt at a sleepover, Mom was also in tears.

She wouldn't tell me why over the phone.

When she picked me up, her eyes were puffy and red. Just like mine. She didn't ask me why I wanted to come home in the middle of the night. Didn't ask why I was crying.

"Your grandmother died," she said.

And everything good and solid in my world disappeared.

9

Now we were returning to Grandma Jeannie's house. Even Josie had to go.

Not that Josie didn't put up a fight. You'd have thought that, given the circumstances, she would have been more understanding. Would have been nicer. But she yelled and screamed when Mom said we were all going to go back to Grandma Jeannie's. She tried to come up with every excuse she could think of, but there was no getting out of it. She was coming to the funeral, and she was going to help us pack Grandma Jeannie's things so Mom could sell the house.

I think *that*, finally, was what convinced Josie

to go: the knowledge that soon, the house would be gone, and she'd never have to go back. Ever. It made me hate her even more. That she could be so happy about something that made me so sad.

I felt like the entire drive was a bad dream.

It was enough to make me forget what happened at the sleepover. Enough to make me forget about dolls or strange events or nightmares.

This was a living nightmare.

Grandma Jeannie was gone.

She was gone, and there was no one else in the world who would listen to me, or understand me.

She was gone.

And so, we were going back. Back to the house and the time I could barely remember.

Back to say good-bye for the last time.

To my grandmother.

To my friend.

And to the only person who could help me with the girl I was starting to become.

10

We drove back from the funeral in silence.

We were wearing black, all three of us, and it was raining hard on the rental car, drowning out the emptiness within. For a little while, I'd been grateful for the rain, because the water dripping from my hair had hidden my tears.

Every time I closed my eyes, I could see the closed black casket and the roses I'd scattered on top of it.

Every time I took a breath, I remembered that Grandma Jeannie was no longer with us.

Mom tried to tell us that Grandma Jeannie was resting now, that she was in a better place, but it didn't feel like that to me. It felt like the end. A horrible, terrible end, and I wanted to kick and scream and cry—anything that would make Grandma Jeannie come back to me.

I knew it wouldn't work. That made it worse.

It didn't help that nothing in the town felt familiar or like home anymore. The only thing that had felt right about this place since we left had been Grandma Jeannie. Without her here, everything felt wrong.

We passed by the post office and the school and the grocery store, and even though it was only four in the afternoon, everything was closed and shuttered. No people walking the streets or even driving past. It was like everyone had taken the day off for Grandma's funeral, although very few had actually shown up. The mayor. A woman with bright red hair who stood at the back and looked vaguely familiar behind her black veil. A librarian. And my mom and Josie and me.

Grandma Jeannie didn't have many friends.

People thought she was strange.

"I can't believe you're making us come back here," Josie said from the back seat. I glared at her from the rearview. She was staring out the window, but her eyes were tight. She'd cried during the funeral, but now she didn't look sad. She looked scared. Under her breath, I heard her whisper, "It isn't safe."

Mom didn't hear her. At least, not the second part.

"Josie," she said patiently, looking in the rearview. "I know coming back is hard on you. It's hard on all of us. But I need you to be supportive, okay? We'll just be here a few days, and then we'll be gone for good." Her voice choked on the last few words. I glanced over to see another tear fall down her cheek.

Josie just looked more miserable. I couldn't tell if she was upset because she'd made Mom cry, or because of what we were about to do.

The idea of going through Grandma's stuff made me feel weird inside. Wrong.

But then, everything about this felt weird and wrong. Grandma Jeannie couldn't be dead. Shouldn't be.

She shouldn't have left me like this.

Mom didn't say anything else, and we were left in an awkward silence. Just the sound of the rain and the swishing of wipers. When we paused at a stop sign, I reached toward the radio knob and turned it on. As I did so, I felt a tingle on the back of my neck.

Like I was being watched.

I turned to look out the window.

And there, on the corner of the street, was the first person I'd seen since leaving the funeral. Standing outside with a big black umbrella tilted to hide his face. Except, when I looked at him, he tilted the umbrella back.

It wasn't a human's face.

It was a doll's.

I gasped, but at that moment, the next song on the radio started to play, drowning out the sound. Mom pulled forward. When I glanced back, it was just a normal guy waiting to cross the street.

Not a doll at all.

"What?" Josie asked. She suddenly seemed on high alert.

"Nothing," I lied. "Just thought I knew him."

I knew she would freak out on me if I mentioned anything about dolls. Josie grumbled something under her breath, but thankfully that, too, was swallowed by the radio.

That wasn't the first time something like that happened. It had been going on for as long as I could remember. It was part of the reason kids at school avoided me—they said I was cursed. Always jumping at nothing, seeing things that weren't there.

Seeing dolls that weren't there.

Whatever it was, it seemed to be happening more and more frequently lately. That, and the nightmares.

"It's only for a few days," Mom said out of nowhere. It sounded like she was trying to reassure herself as much as she was us. "Just a few days of sorting and packing, and then professionals will come in to take care of the rest." She looked over to me. Smiled sadly. "And then we can go home."

I tried to smile back at her. She knew that this place would always be more of a home to me than Chicago, no matter how nice our apartment was.

But when we pulled up the front drive and I stared up at Grandma's big three-story house with its faded wraparound porch, fear lodged in my chest.

It felt like something was waiting for me, deep in the dark shadows of the enormous windows—the windows that had always been filled with light before.

The house looked terribly empty, but that dark presence, that prickling on the back of my neck, told me that we weren't alone.

Mom turned off the car and jumped out, jogging toward the covered porch to avoid as much rain as possible. I put my hand on the door handle and felt a small tingle of electricity. I paused before opening the door.

Surrounding Grandma's house, just past the sweeping lawn, was a forest so thick and tangled, it didn't seem like anyone could pass through it. And yet, the trees seemed alive. Moving and twisting in the wind and rain, as if they were filled with monsters. Or were monsters themselves. I squinted.

Was that something moving in the branches? Something pale and porcelain?

"Do you remember her rules?" Josie asked from the back seat.

I jumped at the sound of her voice.

"I . . ." I couldn't remember, but I didn't want her to know that.

She leaned forward, between the seats, so she was facing me.

"Don't leave the windows open at night," she said. Her voice was heavy.

Memory stirred.

"No dolls in the house," she continued.

The third rule spilled from my lips in time with her words.

"And never, *ever* go to the house in the woods," we said at the same time.

She stared at me knowingly for a long moment, and for the first time in a long time, she didn't say anything mean to me. She just looked deadly serious.

"Don't forget them," she said.

"Girls!" Mom called. Her voice barely carried over the sound of the rain. She waved at us from the front porch. The door was open, and she'd turned the lights on.

"I don't like this," I whispered. The words spilled from my lips before I could stop them.

But rather than making fun of me for being weak, Josie stared at Mom with fear plain on her face.

"Neither do I," she said.

11

"Oh no," Mom whispered.

We stood in the doorway, all three of us, and even though I had been here many times, it didn't look like the same house.

"What happened in here?" Josie asked.

Mom swallowed hard and didn't answer. Instead, she took a step into the living room, gingerly placing her foot so as not to step on anything breakable.

Because the room—no, the *house*—was a complete mess. Papers and photographs were scattered everywhere. Grandma's porcelain collectibles were thrown all over the place. Some of them were shattered; only a few of them were whole. Books had been torn from the shelves, pages ripped and strewn all over. I couldn't see an inch of carpet through the mess.

Even the wallpaper had been ripped off in places.

But that wasn't the worst part. The worst part was the writing.

All over the walls in black and red paint.

All over the papers.

All over the sofa. Even the curtains.

Every. Single. Surface. Was covered in four words:

SHE MUST NEVER RETURN

I looked over to Josie—her mouth was slack as she took it in, all the color drained from her face. She looked like she was in shock. Mom was taking it a little better. She moved deeper into the room, turning on lights, one hand covering her mouth.

I didn't want to step a foot in that room.

This wasn't Grandma Jeannie's house. This wasn't the living room where we'd spent hours talking about daydreams or my school. This wasn't the place that felt like home.

Not anymore.

Had an intruder come in? Someone who hated Grandma Jeannie?

"Did someone rob the place?" I asked. "Should we call the cops?"

Josie shook her head before Mom answered.

"No," Josie whispered. "This was her. That's her handwriting."

"Mom?" I asked. I wanted some reassurance. This couldn't have been Grandma Jeannie's doing. It couldn't.

"Well," Mom finally said. She kept looking around. Her face was stoic. As if she had been prepared for the worst, and it had come at last. "The caretaker did say the place was a mess."

"How could the caretaker have let this happen?" Josie asked angrily. "Isn't that why she was here? To take care of Grandma?"

Mom swallowed and looked at us both for the first time.

"I didn't want to tell you. But when the caretaker called me about . . . about your grandmother's passing, she said that Grandma Jeannie had stolen her key and locked her out for a few days. When she finally came in, she found . . ."

She didn't finish her sentence.

It made me wonder a terrible, horrible thought—where had Grandma Jeannie been when the caretaker found her?

"I didn't think it would be this bad," Mom whispered, almost to herself. She took a deep breath and rolled her shoulders back. "But this place isn't going to pack itself. Let's grab some cleaning supplies and get to work. We can pack once we have some of the mess cleared."

I looked to Josie. Like me, she didn't seem to want to take a step into the house, even though the cold rain and wind hammered behind us. It felt like the house was even more of a storm.

I reached out to take Josie's hand.

Our fingers clasped. Just for a second. Then, like it took her a second to realize what was happening, she shook it off and stepped inside.

I watched her go. My heart dropped.

Then I turned to the words I'd ignored. The ones I couldn't ignore any longer.

SHE MUST NEVER RETURN

Who was Grandma Jeannie talking about? And why, with every single part of my being, did I truly, definitely *not* want to find out?

12

Before we could get to work, Mom wanted to change out of her funeral clothes. Which meant venturing back out into the rain to grab the two suitcases we were splitting between the three of us.

I volunteered to go.

I didn't want to be in the mess of a house any more than I had to. I knew I would have to face it eventually, but maybe a small part of me—no, a large part of me—hoped that when I got back to the house, everything would magically be as I remembered it. The shelves all neatly lined with books and figurines, the lamps glowing cheerfully, a tray of sun tea on the coffee table. And maybe . . . maybe even Grandma Jeannie, sitting in her chair, waiting for me to come in.

It wasn't until I reached the car that I realized I was crying.

Fat, hot tears that poured down my cheeks. I didn't open the door, not at first. Instead, I pressed my forehead against the cold glass and let myself sob, completely unseen and unheard in the pouring rain.

Even though I'd cried when I found out about Grandma, and at the funeral, I hadn't cried like this. It was like a dam burst inside of me, and all my pain and sadness and anger flooded out. Pain, because this was suddenly all very real, even more real than the closed casket lid. Sadness, because I knew I would never, ever see Grandma Jeannie again. And anger, because she had left us like this—left her *house* like this—tarnishing any good memory I might have had of her.

I cried and I cried, and after a few minutes, I felt a new sensation. A tingling on the back of my neck that had nothing to do with the cold water trickling down.

Fear.

I sniffed and forced myself upright.

I felt like I was being watched.

From the woods.

I turned and looked into the shadows there, the tree branches swaying in the wind and the rain, like they were laughing at my hurt. I stared for a long while, not blinking, until my eyes were so blurry I had no choice.

When I did, I saw a flash of movement.

A pale white flutter through the branches.

Not like bird wings. Like limbs. Tiny scuttling limbs.

The fear rose stronger in the back of my throat, and once more the words Grandma had written all over her house came to mind, as if they were burned on the backs of my eyes: *SHE MUST NEVER RETURN.*

I felt like I should know who Grandma Jeannie was talking about. I felt like maybe, in the corners of my memory, I did.

I quickly opened the trunk and grabbed our suitcases.

As I hurried back to the house, I realized my fear wasn't about being watched. Not really.

When I got inside and saw the warnings scrawled all over the house, I knew my fear came from the knowledge that Grandma had spent the last moments of her life terrified something or someone was returning.

And I knew in my gut that whatever it was, if it hadn't come back by now, with Grandma Jeannie gone it would.

Soon.

13

It took us all night to clean.

Mom ordered pizza at one point, but we didn't pause to eat, even though she often tried to make sure we had sit-down dinners together to promote family togetherness. Instead, we cleared off a spot on the dining room table—even the *plates* were broken, and those that weren't had *SHE MUST NEVER RETURN* written all over them—and grabbed slices, eating as we cleaned up the mess Grandma Jeannie had left behind.

Josie had been entirely silent since starting cleaning.

She crouched in a corner of the living room, alone, throwing papers into a large trash bag. I noticed her pause every time she picked up something with Grandma's writing on it. As if she could read more into those four words than either Mom or I could.

When Mom left the room to work in the kitchen, I went over to Josie and bent down by a pile of papers, as if my entire reason for coming over was to help her trash papers. I picked one up, *SHE MUST NEVER RETURN* written on both sides in black ink.

"What do you think it means?" I asked her.

"That Grandma was losing her mind," she replied tightly. She angrily tossed a small dog figurine into the trash. It was one of the few that hadn't broken, but she didn't seem to care.

"You don't mean that," I said.

She looked up at me, and her glare was so angry, so full of hurt, that I actually leaned back.

"Yes, I do. The only good thing about all this mess is that it's going to make it easier to pack things, since most of it's going in the trash now. The sooner we're done, the sooner we can get out of here."

And I caught it. The quick flicker of her eyes as

she looked to the window. To the dark woods beyond the window.

"You know who Grandma Jeannie was writing about," I whispered.

Josie swallowed. I expected her not to answer. Instead, she looked down at the pages she was holding. Her hands trembled.

"How could I forget?" she asked. She looked at me, and tears lined her eyes. "How could *you*?"

I didn't have an answer. Outside, thunder rolled, making both of us jump.

I took the moment to spring to my feet and head into the kitchen to help Mom. Anything to get away from the accusatory glare of Josie, and the questions now warring in my head. What did she mean *I should remember*? And why, when I tried to think of my time here, was it all a blur?

It wasn't until I reached the kitchen that I realized the true reason I had to get away from Josie.

I'd seen her struggle with many emotions in my life.

But I had never seen her so afraid.

14

The emptiness of the house hit like a punch to my gut when it was time to go to bed.

Mom and Josie were going to stay up cleaning, as they were nearly done, but when I started yawning, Mom sent me straight to bed. So I wandered upstairs on my own. Mom had cleaned up here, but the damage hadn't been as bad. I passed by Grandma Jeannie's room. The door was slightly ajar, and I could smell the familiar trace of her perfume, but I hurried on. My speed didn't stop the ache from spreading, or the emptiness from hollowing out my chest. I felt like I couldn't breathe, the weight of loss hurt so bad.

And when I dragged my suitcase into the bedroom I'd slept in off and on for the last few years, I dropped it in shock.

My room had been spared.

Everything in here was tidy and clean, exactly as I had left it. Exactly as I had returned to find it every single visit.

Did Josie know? I didn't think she had been up here. Mom surely knew, but she hadn't said anything. Out of curiosity, I went to the room Josie slept in the last time we'd stayed here. It had been cleaned up, but it was clear that Grandma had still made a mess of the place—although not as bad as downstairs. The books on the shelves were in disarray, and the bed hastily made. I paused in Josie's doorway, staring out at the woods glistening beyond the giant windows.

Memory scratched at the surface along with the branches scratching against the enormous windowpanes. I had slept in here a few times. I remembered that. Remembered coming to Josie to take care of me, to keep me safe. I had been scared of . . . something. Something scratching and calling outside my windows. Coyotes? The wind? Whatever it had been, I knew that Josie had taken care of it.

Now it felt like I couldn't turn to anyone.

Before I could think on it further, I headed back to my room. Maybe I should have felt special that Grandma hadn't torn apart my bookshelves or left strange messages on the walls. In reality, I just felt . . . weird. It was like Grandma Jeannie was singling me out, trying to leave a different message, but no matter how hard I tried, I couldn't figure out what it might be.

I changed into pajamas and hurriedly jumped under the covers, waiting to warm up. As I stared out the window and let sleep close over me, I tried not to think about Grandma Jeannie's warnings, tried not to let myself be afraid.

It would all be over soon, and life would return to normal.

At least, as normal as it could be when the only good thing in my life was gone.

15

I couldn't move.

I stood in the corner of a strange room. A cabin in the woods. A room filled with cobwebs and shadows.

A room filled with dolls.

Hundreds of them.

All of them facing the walls. All, except for the one right before me, with her faded sundress and smudged, triumphant smile. Her porcelain doll skin was cracked in a million places, as if she had been shattered and put back together again.

"*Yesssss,*" hissed a voice beside me. A voice I couldn't see, but that made my insides squirm in fear.

"*You will make a very pretty addition to my collection. You, and your sisterrrr . . .*"

And then I heard it. The front door creaking open. The horrible screech of hinges as someone came in from the forest beyond.

The horrible laugh of the monster beside me as Josie came to my rescue.

I wanted to scream. To tell her to run away. To save herself.

I couldn't move.

Couldn't look away from the smiling doll in front of me.

Couldn't scream.

Not even when the doll walked forward with jagged footsteps. Not even when I heard Josie yell out in fear and the monstrous shadow cackle in triumph.

I couldn't move.

Couldn't save anyone.

The doll moved closer.

Closer—

"Mom says it's time to wake up," Josie said, knocking on my closed door.

I jolted awake, my heart racing so fast I felt it in my throat. Cold sweat dripped off my forehead.

What in the world was that nightmare?

Why did it feel like it had actually happened?

"Come on," Josie said through the door. "Let's go. We've got a lot of work to do."

"I'm coming," I grumbled. "Let me get dressed."

Josie grunted and stomped down the hall.

I flopped back on the bed and looked over to see my reflection in the mirror. Dark shadows ringed my eyes and my hair was a mess, the sheets tangled all around me.

And there, on the nightstand behind me—

the doll from my nightmare, her skin shattered and smudged smile wide.

I yelped and sat bolt upright, turning to grab the doll that I knew beyond any doubt shouldn't be here. Should never have been in here.

But when I looked to the nightstand, she was gone.

17

I didn't catch sight of the doll again all morning, but I could have sworn I saw glimpses of her as we sorted and packed things. Flashes of porcelain and pale sundress at the corner of my eye, darting behind the sofa or climbing up the staircase. Every time, gone before I could truly catch her. Every time, I felt the chill across my skin that always signaled something about to go wrong.

Every time, my eyes snared on the words scrawled everywhere, the warning that only Josie seemed to understand—and refused to talk about.

Eventually, I forced myself to stop looking whenever I thought I saw something move.

Josie was right about one thing—the sooner we were done, the sooner we would be gone. And for the first time in my life, I was starting to want to get out of here as soon as possible.

I didn't really know why we were sorting things for storage anyway. We had a pretty small apartment in Chicago. I couldn't imagine Mom would want us to keep much. Unless she was saving it for us, for the future? It made me consider the items I decided to sort into the "Save" box (for Mom to give a final look-over)—there wasn't much here that I wanted to inherit. Especially since most of it was broken or scribbled on.

A radio played instrumental music in the corner, but it just barely cut over the pounding rain outside. Hours had passed, and none of us had really said a thing to break the silence. What was there to say? I think we all just wanted to get out of here so we could move on, though I knew all our reasons were very different.

"What do you think?" Mom asked Josie. She held

up a tiny porcelain horse. A tiny *pink* porcelain horse. "Wouldn't this look great on your nightstand?"

Josie glanced up from the pile of photo albums she was sorting through and practically growled at the thing.

"That's ugly," she said. "There's no way that's going in my room."

"Josie!" I yelped. "That's rude!"

"What?" Josie asked, rounding on me. "Grandma Jeannie's gone. It's not like I can hurt her feelings. Heck, it's not like she would realize it even if she *was* around. She barely ever knew where she was."

I expected Mom to say something. Anything. Because Josie was completely out of line. Yes, Grandma Jeannie had been losing her memory, but that was no excuse to be so rude about it.

But Mom was clearly not paying attention, or else she just chose to ignore Josie when she was like this. She sighed and gently wrapped the horse in newspaper, then reached for the "Donate" box.

"I think it was hers," she whispered. "From when she was a little girl."

The pain in her words knocked the wind out of me.

"No," I said. "I'll take it. If that's okay."

Mom looked to me as if I was speaking a different language.

"Please?" I asked. I didn't want it, not really, but it clearly hurt Mom to have to give it away. I held out my hand, and after an awkward moment, she handed it over.

Josie mumbled something very not nice under her breath, just loud enough for me to hear but not loud enough to get Mom's attention. I glared at her, my anger rising.

If she didn't want to be here that badly, she could just go. She didn't need to take out her fear or frustration on everyone else.

I was tossing away papers when I saw it. A sheet of paper very different from the rest of the old newspaper clippings.

This one had a drawing on it. One I sort of recognized.

Two girls drawn in crayon, holding hands, surrounded by trees and a rainbow. One of them had brilliant red hair. The other was holding a doll. I recognized the one with a doll immediately as myself. I must have drawn this . . .

So who was the other girl?

A name formed on the tip of my tongue.

Clara.

"Mom?" I asked. "Did I have a friend named Clara?"

At once, the sound of glass shattering filled the room, along with the hiss of the radio as it suddenly turned to loud static.

I jolted and looked over to see Josie staring at me, her eyes wide in scared disbelief. The framed photo she had been sorting lay in shards at her feet.

"Josie! Be careful," Mom warned. She had to yell to be heard above the loud radio static. "Come on, let's get the broom. And, Anna, can you turn off the radio?"

She led Josie out of the room, and I had a feeling I wouldn't get an answer from either of them now. Carefully, making sure to avoid any stray glass, I made my way to the radio.

When I reached the radio, though, I could hear something. Something behind the static.

A woman's voice.

No, *Grandma Jeannie's voice.*

"You must not let her escape," Grandma Jeannie whispered. *"Beryl must never be freed!"*

My finger touched the radio knob.

Before I could even turn it, the radio went dead.

18

Later that night, after Mom went to sleep, I lay awake in bed and stared out the closed window. Rain still battered down outside, which didn't make me feel any more at ease.

Ever since that strange event with the radio, I was feeling . . . off.

No, that wasn't right. I was scared.

The radio thing must have just been some static interference, right?

But then, why did the name Beryl sound so familiar? Why did even *thinking* it fill my veins with ice water?

The last few years had been filled with strange occurrences like that. TVs turning on when I walked by, streetlamps flickering off when we drove under them. And the dolls. Always the dolls. Whispering when I walked by. Turning their heads when I wasn't looking at them straight on. Moving when my back was turned. Things I should have been scared by, but had almost been comforting in a way. After all, dolls had been my friends. Friends I had to keep secret, for fear of what my sister or school friends would say.

I had convinced myself that it was just my *overactive imagination*, as Mom called it, and that if I ignored it, the strange things would stop happening. Except now, it seemed, they were getting more frequent. Ever since we got into town.

Almost like this place was the cause of it all.

Almost like it was calling me back.

"*Anna,*" a voice whispered.

My eyes jolted open.

Had I fallen asleep? It wouldn't be the first time I'd had a dream so intense I was convinced it was real. I'd even sleepwalked, on occasion.

I sat there, my heart pounding, and the only noise

was the pounding rain outside. I wanted to tell myself it had just been a dream, but the fear was real and stuck to me like sweat.

I took a deep, calming breath. I must have fallen asleep without knowing—that voice almost sounded like . . .

"*Anna,*" a voice whispered, followed by a soft tapping at my door.

My fear turned to agitation as I realized who it was. I slid from bed and made my way over. When I cracked the door open, Josie stuck her head in and looked around. That was strange. She never came into my room at night. It had always been *me* going to *her.*

"Good," she muttered after looking around. She pushed the door open the rest of the way and stepped inside.

"What?" I asked, ruffled. Because I wasn't entirely certain it was her voice the first time I heard my name whispered. Maybe I'd been falling asleep after all. "What's good?"

"Your windows are closed," she said.

I looked to the windows.

Of *course* they were closed—it was still raining out there and it was freezing. I didn't say that, though. I just mumbled in agreement.

She walked over to a window, and that's when I realized what seemed the most off. She seemed even more afraid than before.

"What is it?" I asked as she peered out the window to the forest beyond.

She didn't answer right away. She just stared out the window as if entranced, one hand pressed to the glass. I stepped up to her and looked out. Through the rain, I could just make out the swaying black trees of the forest beyond in the porch light. And yes, it was night, and it was raining, but something about the way the tree limbs moved, the way the shadows darted about, made the forest seem . . . alive.

I felt myself swaying back and forth with the motion of the trees. They were hypnotizing. They were calling to me . . .

I bumped against Josie, and she broke from her trance.

"Watch it, weirdo," she said. She took a step back and shook her head, as if shaking off a dream.

"What?" I asked. *Why are you acting so strange? What do you know that you aren't telling me?*

But of course I didn't ask her those things. She would never have answered even if I'd tried.

"Just make sure you keep your windows shut," she said. "And don't go out to the house in the woods. It's not . . . it's not safe."

She turned and headed out my door, but the words I heard on the radio whispered through my head.

"Does it have to do with Beryl?" I asked.

She froze.

She didn't move for the longest time, and when she did, her eyes were wide and rimmed with tears.

"Don't you ever, *ever* mention that name again, you hear me? Never!" Her last word came out as a hissed yell, and before I could promise anything, she slammed the door in my face and thundered down the hall.

I stood there and watched the door, feeling hot and cold all at the same time.

She knew.

She knew about Beryl, which maybe meant she knew what was going on around here—the writing on the walls, the strange rules, and even Grandma Jeannie's voice on the radio.

And there was no doubt in my mind that Josie would never tell me. Tears welled in my eyes. If Grandma Jeannie was here, I could ask her. But if she was here, none of this would be happening in the first place.

Once more, I felt more alone than ever before.

Frustrated, I slipped back under my covers and closed my eyes.

Josie was keeping secrets. Josie was scared of something out here. Of something or some*one* named Beryl.

The name tugged at my memory, but I couldn't remember anything. I knew it had to do with the time we had lived here. I knew it had to do with Grandma and the strange messages and my nightmares. And even though I was right here, in the place it had all happened, I couldn't remember a thing.

As sleep slid in, I heard a scratching on my window.

Porcelain on glass.

The scratch of tiny doll hands.

19

I jumped at the sound, suddenly fully awake, and stared out the window.

I couldn't see anything. No branches clawing at the glass.

No tiny dolls scratching to get in.

Although a part of me wanted to hide back under my covers, the rest of me had to be sure. Had to be sure I wasn't being watched. Had to be sure I wasn't making this up.

Trembling, clutching the blanket to my chest, I made my way to the window.

Lightning flashed outside, illuminating the

driveway and the garden and the forest beyond. I leaned forward and squinted. Was that . . . ?

Yes, farther out in the woods, was a glow. The faint orange glow of a window, and a trail of spiraling smoke, and I knew without doubt in that moment that *that* was the house I was supposed to avoid.

That was where Beryl lived. Though how I knew that in the core of my bones was beyond me.

I leaned closer to the window and tried to peer out.

I placed my hand on the cold glass.

And a tiny porcelain hand slapped against it on the other side.

I yelped and leaped back, staring in horror as a doll clambered its way up to peer in the window at me.

A doll with a smudged smile and a thousand cracks and a faded sundress.

Memory flashed with the lightning.

I remembered holding a doll tight to my chest while falling asleep, a secret for me alone. A doll given to me by Josie's only friend in town.

Vanessa.

This was the doll Vanessa had given me. How could I have forgotten Josie's only friend?

The tiny porcelain fist pounding against the window brought me back to the present.

A crack appeared in the glass. It was going to break in!

Another thud—how was no one hearing this? why was no one coming in to save me?—and the crack grew wider.

I could hear the doll laughing now. I could hear her whisper in my thoughts.

Beryl wants what was stolen. Beryl is coming for you!

I yelped as her fist cracked through the glass, sending shards scattering over the wooden floor.

I took a step back.

She stuck her head through the hole. Her hair dripped water to the floor.

"You can't run," she hissed. *"You were already hers!"*

I turned to flee, but I only got halfway around before freezing. I couldn't move my legs. I couldn't move my arms.

I looked down at my feet in horror to see them turning to porcelain.

And when I looked into the mirror, I watched in

horror as my face leeched of color, my skin smoothing out and my eyes becoming pale marbles. I was turning into a doll!

I tried to open my mouth to scream, but my lips couldn't move. I couldn't move at all.

I was a doll!

I tilted.

Tipped.

And as I fell toward the floor, the doll from the window cackled with Beryl's terrifying laughter.

I hit the ground, screaming silently.

I shattered—

And woke up with a start.

Sheets tangled my feet and sweat coated my forehead and I lay on my back on the floor. I stared over at my bed in shock. I'd been dreaming. I was having another nightmare. But this one had felt so *real*.

When I looked to the window, the glass was intact. A branch scratched against it. Had that been what I'd heard? Was that what gave me the nightmare?

I pushed myself up to standing and briefly looked into the mirror. I wasn't a doll. Of course I wasn't a doll.

So why did it feel like—at one point—I had been for real?

When I curled back into bed, I hoped against hope that I would fall back asleep. That I wouldn't have any nightmares.

But the night wore on, and the storm continued, and the tree scratched at the window, and every time I started to drift, I heard a whisper.

I heard a woman calling my name.

And even though I could no longer see it, I knew it was coming from the cabin in the woods.

20

When the sun finally rose and I heard Mom shuffling around downstairs, I peeled myself out of bed and made my way to the bathroom to try and wash some of the sleepiness from my face. But no matter how much cold water I splashed on my cheeks, I couldn't make myself feel awake. Every step felt like a half dream. My movements felt like they were through water.

Even though it had only been one night, it felt like I hadn't slept in weeks.

Every time I blinked, I thought I wouldn't be able to open my eyes again.

Every time I glanced into a mirror, I expected to see a doll staring back in my place.

What in the world was happening to me?

For a split second, I thought of going to ask Grandma Jeannie for help. She would know what was going on. Or, at least, she wouldn't think I was crazy.

Then I remembered that she was gone. I'd never be able to talk to her again. I'd never be able to ask her for help or advice.

I was alone.

Before I could stop myself, I leaned against the sink and started to cry.

21

"You look like a zombie," Josie said when I finally got downstairs.

I'd spent a good five minutes crying against the sink, and when I was done, I took a shower because my eyes were red and puffy and I didn't want anyone commenting on it. I didn't want Josie's snark or Mom's concern.

Apparently it didn't work.

Not that Josie had much room to talk—she had dark circles under her eyes. Was she having nightmares, too? It wasn't something I dared ask.

Mom wasn't in the kitchen. She was already over in the living room, packing up more boxes.

I poured myself a bowl of cereal and slumped down. Even the cereal tasted strange.

"What's gotten into you?" Josie asked. She was sorting plates and bowls into boxes. Most of them were going into the "Donate" box. At least, the ones not broken

I wondered if she remembered Vanessa. Was Vanessa even around? If so, why wasn't Josie trying to hang out with her old friend?

"Couldn't sleep," I responded.

"Did you keep your windows closed?"

I glanced up at her.

"Yes. Why?"

She shrugged. "The rules."

"Why do you care about the rules?" I asked. "I'm surprised you're not breaking all of them now that Grandma's dead!"

Josie glowered at me. I turned my gaze to my cereal, because I knew what I'd said had gone too far.

"Her rules kept us safe," she said quietly. She swallowed. "Until *you* broke them."

"What are you talking about?" I asked.

I could tell that was pushing her too far. I fully

expected her to yell at me. Instead, she looked to the room where Mom was packing and took a deep breath.

"You wouldn't understand," she said. She didn't try to explain. After another awkward moment, she stomped from the room and went to help Mom.

I sat there and glumly ate my cereal. Maybe I should ask her about Vanessa. See if that got her to open up about what was happening.

Then I heard Mom start crying about something she found, and I knew all my questions would have to wait for another time.

22

Josie avoided me for the rest of the morning. I kept trying to corner her to ask a question, but she avoided me at every chance. Either that, or she stayed close to Mom. It was clear I'd rattled her, just as it was clear that I wasn't going to learn anything else from her. I still wanted to know about Clara and Vanessa, but Mom was in no state to answer questions—she had been crying after finding a bunch of her baby pictures. I didn't want to push her.

The hours dragged on in silence. I didn't trust turning the radio on again, and no one was talking, which meant I spent the time asking myself the same questions over and over, as if I might eventually shake out an answer. I couldn't.

By the time Mom said that she and Josie were going to go drop off some stuff at the donation center in town, I was ready to explode with frustration. I still couldn't remember anything else about Clara or Vanessa or Beryl, save for a vague assurance that they had existed. I helped Mom load a few big boxes into the back of Grandpa's old beat-up pickup truck. Mom asked if I wanted to come with them. But the thought of having to sit between Josie and Mom for a long, bumpy ride into town sounded like the last thing I wanted to do. I would rather be alone.

That's what I was used to being. And it was clear neither of them wanted me around anyway.

I watched them drive off from the front porch. Last night's storm had turned into a lovely, sunny summer day. Even the woods no longer looked as creepy as they did the night before. It should have been pretty, but the moment the truck disappeared around the corner, a great heavy weight settled on my shoulders.

The weight of emptiness. The knowledge that

Grandma wasn't going to step out beside me with sun tea and more stories.

It felt like the big house behind me was settling on my shoulders, all dust and wood and secrets. I knew if I went back inside, it would suffocate me.

I had to stay outside.

I had to walk.

I trudged around to the back of the house. The old play set was still back there but badly weathered and probably no longer stable. It felt like forever ago that Josie and I had played there, the memories such a blur I could almost believe it never happened. Back when we had truly been sisters. Friends. So much had changed . . .

I glanced over to the garden. More half memories stirred at the sight of the sunflowers poking up from the weeds. Once, the garden had been lovingly tended, but now it was all overgrown. All of it except for a single patch of black dirt. My eyes snared on that spot. Something about it felt wrong, but I couldn't put my finger on why.

I growled in frustration. Everything about this

place was like the memory of a dream. Why couldn't I remember anything? Why did a part of me not *want* to remember anything? I was getting so frustrated I nearly turned around and stormed back inside— maybe I could find a book or something to take my mind off why nothing seemed to make sense anymore.

And then I saw it. The most beautiful blue butterfly I'd ever seen. It fluttered off the back porch and danced around my head before floating lightly over to the edge of the yard.

Where it landed lightly on a tree. Fluttering its wings as if waiting for me.

I glanced around. Mom and Josie were out of sight and wouldn't be back for hours at least—the donation center was in the next town over. Josie's warning floated through my head: *Don't go to the house in the woods.*

It was Grandma's rule, and I knew it had been to keep us safe. But I needed answers. I needed to know if she truly had just been losing her mind, or if there was something that we needed to be kept safe from. And the only way to find out was to seek it out myself.

I took a step toward the woods. The butterfly took

off from its bough, fluttering down a path I could just barely see through the underbrush.

A chill raced over the back of my neck, and for a split second, I swore I could smell Grandma Jeannie's perfume. It felt like she was there. Warning me. Telling me not to go into the woods.

Immediately, a pang of sadness speared my heart. But then a new emotion took over. Anger.

"You left me alone here," I whispered to the wind. "You said you would always be there for me. But you left me. This is all your fault."

A cool breeze swept around me, and the scent of her perfume faded, leaving only the smell of wet grass and warming leaves. Blue butterfly wings flashed in the woods.

Before I could change my mind, I followed the butterfly in.

23

It dropped ten degrees the moment I stepped under the cool canopy of the trees.

Honestly, it felt like entering a completely new world. The sound of wind was replaced with the chirping of birds and rustling of squirrels in the branches. Bugs buzzed happily about, weaving in and out of the sunlight piercing the foliage above. And ahead of me, the blue butterfly floated serenely, always a few steps ahead on the path.

I followed.

With every step, my frustration and sadness lessened, until everything seemed like a distant memory.

Josie, Mom, Chicago, even losing Grandma Jeannie—they were all replaced by the calm I felt in the woods.

Why were we not supposed to be out here? This place felt *magical*.

I didn't know how long I walked, but eventually the butterfly fluttered high up into the trees. I watched it go, both sad and entranced as it flew into the sunlight.

When I looked back down, I found the house.

It was like staring at a nightmare incarnate, and whatever joyous feelings I'd had before vanished at the sight of it.

The yard was completely overgrown with stunted trees and vines that twined around broken concrete bird feeders and tumbled mounds of stone. The house itself was decrepit, with a sagging roof and broken windows that gaped with an inky blackness that sent shivers through my limbs.

And even though I knew that a place this old, this abandoned, should smell like must and moss and decay, the breeze that seemed to waft from the front door carried the unmistakable scent of baking chocolate chip cookies.

I had been here before. I knew it. Just as I knew that, tangled and overgrown as the front yard was, it was missing something. I just couldn't remember *what*.

I don't know why I did it. Even as bad memories tugged at the corners of my awareness, I walked toward the front door, which fell inward on broken hinges like a tired mouth. The scent of baking pulled me forward, even though the memories pulled me back: I knew I should be afraid of this place. I knew— Grandma's rules or no—that this was the last place I should want to be.

But I was captivated.

Something pulled me. An energy. A gravity. And I couldn't choose to turn away, even if I wanted to.

I didn't want to.

This was a secret. This was a way to get back at Josie, to show her I wouldn't be bullied anymore. I was going to do exactly what she told me not to. *Then* she'd learn not to push me around.

Gingerly, quietly, I stepped past the front door. The floor sunk dangerously under my foot, but it didn't give way. Every step caused a creak that echoed through the hallway and raised the hairs on the back of my neck.

The scent of baking was stronger in here, but there wasn't any sound. It didn't look like anyone had been in here for years. Only rats.

Spiderwebs stretched from floor to ceiling, and dust lay heavy on the shelves lining the walls. Empty shelves.

For some reason, that scared me. Hadn't there been something on those shelves before?

Memory flashed.

Dolls.

This hall had once been lined with hundreds of dolls. All shapes and sizes, in all styles of dress. All of them facing the walls. All of them silent, so silent it was practically a scream. And that was what had been missing from the front yard. There had been doll heads piled in the bird feeders and giant doll bodies twined with vines in the bushes. Dolls had been everywhere. Broken. Shattered. Or eerily whole.

So where were they now? The question should have been enough to send me running.

Memories kept tugging—I should *know* this, I

should—but the gravity tugged harder, and I walked farther down the hallway. Light peeked through cracks in the walls or the broken windows, dappling the floor in patchy sunlight. The shadows were strangely thick, puddled like oil.

They could have been hiding anything.

Near the end, I stopped.

Something was on the ground. Right in the middle of the hall, hidden in shadow, as if it had been placed there just for me to discover.

A rock? A piece of caved-in ceiling?

I bent down to investigate, even as a small, rational part of my brain screamed to run far, far away.

The light shifted, and my breath caught in my throat as I realized what was waiting for me.

A doll.

24

The doll was definitely no cute child's toy.

She wore a dress that appeared to be nothing but long tattered strands of black fabric, and the hands that poked from the sleeves of her dress had elongated fingers tipped in sharp black nails. Her black hair hung lank and gnarled around a pale porcelain face. Her eyes were black voids that scratched out to the edges like witchy black eye shadow, with tiny pinpricks of white in the center where pupils should be. And her smile . . . it wasn't a friendly smile, but a fang-flecked sneer.

As if she were feeling triumphant. As if she had succeeded in something terrible.

I didn't want to know what it could be.

Worse, something about the doll was familiar . . . I tried to think back, but my memories lodged against a wall of forgetting. I knew I should know about the doll, but I couldn't remember. How could I forget something this terrifying?

"Who are you?" I whispered.

I looked around. There was no one here, that was for sure. My footsteps were the only ones on the dusty floorboards. Stranger still, everything in the house was covered in dust and cobwebs—everything, that was, except for her.

She looked clean and new, even if her clothes were ragged and her hair a mess.

I don't know why I did it—it was the same gravity that pulled me to and into the house in the first place.

I reached out and touched her cheek.

It was warm.

Lights flashed behind my eyes.

Lights and a swirl of shadow and a scream, a high-pitched scream that made my eyes roll to the back of my head. And in the flickering, flashing lights, in the feeling of a thousand needles poking into my skin and the world falling away as I shrunk to the floor, I saw a face.

I saw Josie's face.

Then the lights and the shadows overwhelmed me, the floor and room spinning out of control. I stumbled, reached out for the wall.

And when the nausea cleared and I managed to right myself, the terrifying doll was gone.

25

I groggily pushed myself to standing, holding myself up against the wall to keep from falling as the whole room tilted, or maybe I tilted, I wasn't certain. I squeezed my eyes shut and took deep breaths, counting slowly to ten.

When I opened my eyes, the doll was still missing, and the deserted house no longer smelled like baking—now it smelled like must and decay, and I wanted nothing more than to get out of there as fast as I could.

I wobbled my way down the hall, keeping one

hand out for balance and trying not to need it—the last thing I wanted was to brush against a cobweb, or worse, a giant fuzzy spider. Just the thought made me shudder. As did the question: Was the doll still in here, hiding in the shadows, waiting for me . . . or was she a part of my imagination, just as all of Grandma Jeannie's warnings had been part of hers?

I made my way out of the hall and into the cool afternoon air. Any moment, I expected the doll to leap from the shadows and attack me. The creeping silence was almost worse. I *knew* there had once been broken doll parts out here. Where had they gone? Who had taken them?

I took a deep breath of fresh air and slowly made my way to the path back to Grandma Jeannie's. Once I was out of the yard, I paused and looked back to the abandoned house.

A shadow darted from the window, disappearing deep within.

Chills raced down my neck, and my stomach turned over. I knew what I had seen, even though I refused to believe it.

The nightmarish doll that had been waiting for me in the shadows.

She had been watching from the window.

And she hadn't been alone.

26

"Where the heck were you?" Josie growled when I got back to Grandma's yard.

She and Mom were already home, but whereas it looked like Mom had gone back inside to continue packing, Josie was on the back porch. Waiting for me.

"I was—"

She stormed off the porch and grabbed my shoulder. Hard.

"Don't you dare lie to me," she hissed. She looked in my eyes as she spoke. I looked down to my shoes.

"You went to her house, didn't you?" she accused.

"I—"

"I can't believe you!" she yelled. "Do you have any idea what you've done? I can't believe you! You are just. So. Stupid!"

Tears welled in my eyes and fell down my cheeks.

"I'm not stupid," I said, grateful I was able to get out at least one full sentence.

"You have no idea what you've done," she whispered. She looked past me, toward the woods. "I've done everything I could to protect you. Everything! And you've blown it. Again! Whatever happens, Anna, I want you to remember that it's all your fault."

She pushed me away, then turned and stormed back into the house.

I couldn't move. All I could do was stand there, sniffing back tears, trying to convince myself that I hadn't actually done anything wrong.

No one had been in the creepy house. Nothing bad happened.

But the doll . . . She was waiting for you. She was watching. And now that she's seen you . . .

Despite the warmth of the afternoon sun, chills raced down my spine, and I turned to face the shadowed woods, positive I felt eyes on the back of my neck.

Nothing there.

I squared my shoulders and headed to the back door.

When I touched the doorknob, I heard it.

A rustling.

A whisper.

I turned back to the empty forest.

No, no, I had to be imagining it.

There was no one there.

No one there.

I opened the screechy back door.

So . . . who had been calling my name?

27

Sorting through Grandma's things was even harder with Josie glaring at me. She didn't say anything, not with Mom there, but she didn't have to. I could feel her disappointment everywhere I turned. Whenever I passed her, she would whisper terrible things under her breath, insults that made me feel worse than I had before. Finally, I couldn't take it anymore and excused myself to go work upstairs. On my own.

Someone had to sort out Grandma Jeannie's room. I might as well start.

I made sure to lock her door behind me. I didn't want Josie or Mom coming in.

The moment the door closed, I leaned against it and sighed in relief. Like my room, this one hadn't been touched by Grandma's rampage. It was exactly as I'd remembered it.

The bed was still made, with the handmade quilt pulled tight. The long drapes were tied back to let in the afternoon sun, which glinted on her bureau lined with photographs and old perfume bottles.

The room even smelled like her, a dusty floral scent that immediately made me feel a little better.

I took another deep breath.

It felt like she was still here with me. I liked that. It made me feel safe.

I took a step forward and placed a gentle hand on her bed. I didn't sit down on it. For some reason, that felt wrong. Rude.

"I wish you were still here," I whispered. Tears welled in my eyes again. "I don't know what's going on anymore. Everything seems so wrong. I wish . . . I wish you were here to tell me everything would be okay."

Something clicked behind the bureau. I jolted and turned around. The scent of Grandma's perfume was stronger, but the room was empty. Except . . .

Hesitantly, I walked over to the bureau. I could feel a draft coming out from behind it. Could it be . . . ?

I pressed my hands to the bureau and pushed against it—the big piece of furniture slid easily, and it was then that I realized it was on tiny rollers. It slid a few feet right along the wall without a sound.

And there, in the wall, was a crack of flickering light.

I peered closer.

Behind the bureau was a hidden door, maybe four feet high and perfectly hidden behind the furniture. A hidden room.

Why did Grandma Jeannie have a hidden room?

For a moment, I considered running downstairs and telling Mom. But part of me knew that this was meant for me alone, even though I couldn't understand why.

I reached for the door and opened it slowly. Grandma Jeannie's perfume wafted out, as if trying to convince me that this was okay, that I was meant to be in here.

When I stepped in and let the door close behind me, I gasped in amazement.

The room was beautiful.

The floor had been painted a deep black, and tiny silver stars glittered across it in a collection of constellations that continued up the walls, the background fading from black to light blue. The ceiling was pale blue and purple, like a dawn sky, with even more stars scattered about and swaths of paint spiraling around like the Milky Way. It felt like standing in the middle of the cosmos. A dozen candles burned brightly all around me, some dripping on the floor or on tall iron pillars, while others hung from the ceiling in crystal sconces.

Herbs hung along one wall, dangling from pale silver thread as they dried, and low shelves lined the other walls, some holding old books and others holding jars of crushed herbs or glittering potions. And right across from me was a low steamer trunk with a plush blue velvet cloth draped over it. Two candles flanked a large leather book in the center.

A folded notecard sat on top of the book. Waiting for me.

Entranced, I knelt down in front of the trunk and reached for the note. Maybe it was my imagination, but the note seemed warm and the book seemed to tingle under my touch. When I unfolded the note, Grandma Jeannie's perfume wafted pleasantly over me, and all my old frustration washed away.

My dearest Anna,

By now you've realized you're not like other girls.

You have a gift. One stronger than even mine.

I only wish I could have taught you how to use it. I wanted to. Dearly. But I feared telling you the truth.

I didn't want to take your childhood from you.

Once you realize the power within you, there is no turning back. There is no protecting you from those who would take your power for their own. But then, there is no hiding from yourself either.

I can only hope this book will help in my absence.

I love you, always.

Grandma Jeannie.

28

For a while, I could only sit there, staring at the note, reading it over and over to make sure I hadn't misunderstood.

Grandma Jeannie said I had a power. Memories churned—the dolls, the voices, the *sleepover*—and they all seemed to swirl around the old leather book in front of me.

I folded the note back up and slipped it in my pocket. Then I carefully opened the leather book. The moment my fingers touched the cover, a warm current of electricity shimmered through me. It almost felt like a cat purring.

Inside the book were a bunch of strange and wonderful things that didn't make much sense: star charts and almanacs; sketches of herbs and all their attributes, like increasing luck or curing colds; long poems in Latin that almost looked like . . . spells?

My heart started hammering wildly, and my fingers shook.

I paused and put the book down, looking up and around the small room.

For the first time since the funeral, things were starting to make sense. All the long talks with Grandma Jeannie about the nature of the universe, and the language of birds and other animals. The strange currents of energy I often felt. She said she had heard and felt all of them, too. Said that for women like us, that was perfectly normal. Natural.

Is this what she meant? She was a witch, and I was one, too?

Perhaps that was why this room felt so comfortable. So safe. Even with its unknown dried herbs and bottles of potions and glittering, glowing constellations. In here, everything I'd wondered about was made into reality. In here, my fantasies were just facts of life. Ones that Grandma Jeannie had known about.

And written about.

My head began to ring as I skimmed through the rest of the pages. More star charts, more recipes, more beautiful drawings of plants with all their properties. I felt like I'd been spinning around too fast. My vision blurred as I read, and I could feel something trying to claw its way into my thoughts. Memories from my past. Things I wanted to keep locked away. Memories that *needed* to stay locked away.

One page in particular caught my attention.

On it was an inky portrait of a monstrous woman with jet-black hair and robes, her eyes blazing white. It looked a great deal like the doll I had seen in the cabin in the woods. Below it was a block of text.

All these years I have contained Beryl's evil to the house in the woods. Her magic springs from that cursed place, and no matter how hard I try, I cannot end it. Even after her supposed defeat, I sense the magic emanating from that house. I have tried burning or tearing it down, but a supernatural force keeps all efforts from succeeding. The best I can do is contain the power there for as long as I can. But I'm growing weak. Soon, I will be gone, and when I am, I fear that Beryl will return. I wish I could be there to stop her. I wish I knew how. After a life of trying to end her evil, I have done nothing but postpone it for another to handle. When she comes back, she will be limited to the woods so long as my spell holds. But it will not hold forever, and she cannot be released into the world.

I stared at the figure on the page. Her eyes seemed to pull me in, her mouth widening in a monstrous, animal sneer. A great ringing filled my ears, threatening to give me a headache as memories banged against the walls of my mind, trying to get in. Trying to be remembered. The light of the candles seemed to dim as memory pressed back in. Like a great swelling ocean wave, rising up to take me over, the words on the page overcame my senses, threatened to pull me under, to drown me, and through it all, I swore I heard Grandma Jeannie's voice, warning me, calling me, afraid for me, and a terrifying cackle, coming from the woods—

I closed the book and set it back on the trunk. Instantly, the room came back into focus. I sat there, my breathing heavy, and listened hard. I could have sworn I heard someone calling me. Could have sworn I was no longer alone in the room. But as I sat there and my breathing slowed, I realized I was still alone. Mom and Josie were still clanging around downstairs. Whatever I'd heard had been in my imagination.

I considered bringing the book with me, hiding it in my room so I could read more of it later. But I didn't want to risk anyone else finding it. Especially if Josie decided to root around in my room. If Grandma Jeannie had been able to keep this room secret for so long, chances were good I could keep it secret for a few days more.

The question was, would I want to come back here? Or did I want to keep all those bad memories locked safely away? Grandma Jeannie said I had a power, said this book could help me. But when I thought of everything the strange power within me had done, using it again was the last thing I wanted to do. All it had done was get me in trouble. It had hurt my friends. Maybe Josie was right about everything—maybe we should just get out of here as soon as we could and leave all of Grandma Jeannie's secrets and stories far behind us, where they couldn't hurt us. Whoever Beryl was, she was probably just a figment of Grandma's imagination—there was nothing in the world as terrifying as the creature on the page. It just *couldn't* be real.

I hoped.

So why did it feel like she was just as real as Josie or me?

Chills raced down my spine at the thought of a monster like the one Grandma had drawn prowling the woods. *That* I know I would have remembered.

Suddenly scared, I stood and turned to go.

As I did, all the candles in the room flickered, and this time I knew it wasn't my imagination.

"Be careful," Grandma Jeannie warned. *"Beryl is watching you."*

29

It was impossible to focus the rest of the afternoon.

I quickly left Grandma's bedroom and—even though it meant being next to Josie—went downstairs to help Mom pack up. After making sure the bureau was safely hiding the hidden door again, of course. I didn't want Josie coming upstairs to check on what I'd been doing and discovering my secret.

"What were you doing up there?" Josie growled. "You weren't breaking any of the rules, were you?"

"No," I said quietly. "I was just avoiding *you*."

Josie's jaw dropped. I don't think I'd ever talked back to her before.

Before she could retaliate, I turned and went next to Mom to help her sort through Grandma's fine china. I didn't know where my nerve came from. Maybe I was just tired of feeling like everyone was keeping things from me, even though I knew I was the one keeping them—somehow—from myself.

I was trying to concentrate on sorting cups and plates and all that, but I kept thinking about Grandma's secret room.

What other secrets had Grandma Jeannie been keeping from me?

What was it that I couldn't remember?

And why was it that she was only warning me about Beryl now, after she was gone, rather than when she was alive and able to help?

Then Josie walked in and looked at the stacks of dishes.

"I bet she forgot she even had half of this stuff," she muttered.

Which brought another thing to mind . . .

Grandma Jeannie had been forgetting more and more in her final years, and there were times she didn't seem to be there at all. When she was coherent, she was my best friend. But when she wasn't, she was like a different person altogether.

She was almost scary.

Yelling about nonsense. Creatures in the woods trying to get in. Dolls attacking the house. Or else words and phrases that weren't even English, or any language I'd ever heard.

Josie had rudely said Grandma Jeannie was losing her mind, hearing things that weren't there, thinking that fantasy was real. What if *Josie* was the one telling the truth?

What if . . . what if *that's* how Grandma Jeannie and I were similar?

What if this was all made up? What if Grandma Jeannie had just constructed some elaborate fantasy, a world where there were witches and monsters and creepy dolls? What if the house in the woods was just an abandoned house that creeped Grandma out? What if the spellbook and hidden room and all that stuff about having powers were just more pieces of Grandma's fantasy world, stories she'd cooked up when she wasn't thinking straight?

And what if, in believing it, I was destined to lose my mind as well?

Even though the thought was scary, the alternative was even worse: If this *was* real, it meant we really were in danger.

And it was somehow up to me to stop it.

30

I wanted to go back to Grandma's secret room all evening, but I never got the chance. Mom went up and started cleaning out Grandma Jeannie's closet. I kept waiting for her to call out that she'd found something, but she never did, which made me think that maybe the hidden room truly was a secret just for me.

Josie stopped being mean, at least for now, but she glared at me whenever we made eye contact.

It was bedtime before I was finally alone again. Crickets chirped outside my closed bedroom window.

It was stifling in here. Last night's storm had made everything outside wet, and the sun today was hot and the air inside was humid and like an oven, and Grandma Jeannie didn't have AC. I was lying on top of the sheets and was still coated in sweat. Gross.

I'd never be able to sleep like this.

Even though Josie had warned me not to, I went over to the windows and opened both of them, letting in a cool night breeze. Instantly, the sound of crickets grew louder. Louder than traffic in Chicago ever had. It was soothing, in a way.

It made me think that nothing bad could ever truly happen here—it was too peaceful. Grandma had always said the natural world was magic, so why should I shut it out?

I stared out at the woods beyond. In the moonlight, even they looked harmless. I could almost imagine the abandoned house out there, moonlight glinting on the doll fragments and overgrown vines in the front yard. I shuddered at the thought.

Maybe not *everything* out there was harmless.

Before my imagination could get the better of me, I slipped into bed. It was still too hot for covers, but at least the breeze was cooling me down. I looked over to the pink horse figurine I'd rescued from donations.

It made me think of Grandma, playing with it as a little girl. Just like I had played with my dolls.

"I wish you were here," I whispered to Grandma's memory. It felt like I'd been wishing that a lot lately.

As exhaustion pulled me under, I heard a scratching on my window. I didn't open my eyes.

It was just a branch in the breeze. It wasn't porcelain fingers.

Just a branch . . .

Just a . . .

31

In the darkness of my dream, I heard her cackling.

Beryl's laughter filled my ears and vibrated my bones as I stood in that creepy back room of her house, towers of books all around me and a pedestal beside me.

"You will be a fine addition to my collection," she said to me. "And once I have your sister, your grandmother will have no choice but to release me from this prison, and my collection will grow ever more!"

I wanted to scream. Wanted to run away from this creepy house with dolls on every surface, dolls with crossed-out eyes and silent screams on their painted lips. But I couldn't move. Beryl had paralyzed me, and all I could do was stand there, fear coursing through my veins as I stared up at her terrifying visage.

She didn't look like a woman.

No, her face and ears had elongated, stretched out like a bat's, and shadows seemed to writhe around her like serpents, twining through her tattered dress, dripping from her gnarled hair. Her eyes glowed bright white, like two full moons in the dead, dark night. She was a creature from my deepest, darkest nightmares, and she had me trapped.

All because of Clara, who stood beside me with her hands clasped before her chest, pleading.

Clara, with her bright red hair and frilly dress.

Clara, who had said she was my friend. Who had invited me here. Who had led me straight into the trap by trying to get me to turn on my sister and family.

I knew my family would never find me. They probably wouldn't even come looking for me. Clara might have been lying about everything else, but she'd been telling the truth about one thing: My family didn't want me around.

"And then you'll release me?" Clara asked.

"Of course, Clara," Beryl said. "But first, I must work my magic on this one." She took a step closer and reached into her pocket, and I closed my eyes in fear. I wanted to step back. But I couldn't. I couldn't do anything. "Don't worry, little one. This will hurt a *great* deal."

Something looped around my neck.

It felt like fire ants crawling all over my skin, burning and biting, while being zapped with electricity. And as my fingertips turned to porcelain, I was finally able to scream.

32

I woke up covered in sweat. Birds chirped in the clear morning sunshine, but I didn't feel refreshed. I didn't feel safe. I felt like I'd spent all night running from a nightmare. A nightmare of Beryl. Of dolls.

Not just dolls. Being *turned into* a doll.

The memories of my time here flooded back in a rush.

I remembered the first few days here, right at the start of the school year, when it had seemed like nothing Josie or I could do would make us fit in. The kids at school had been mean to me. Horribly mean. Just as they'd been mean to Josie.

Coming back to Grandma Jeannie's house hadn't made anything better—she'd been getting worse and worse, her stories of the monstrous Beryl filling my dreams with nightmare. More often than not, I'd slept in Josie's room for fear of the voices I could hear from the woods outside. Voices calling both our names.

It had seemed like this was the worst experience of our lives, and Josie and I had wanted nothing but to return to Chicago.

Until Josie met Vanessa. The coolest girl in school. She'd even been nice to me. Had gifted me a doll in a sundress to keep me safe from nightmares. At the time, Josie found Grandma Jeannie's three rules—*don't open the windows at night, no dolls in the house, and never, ever go to the house in the woods*—as strange as I did. Josie was the one who said it was okay to keep the doll. To hide it from Grandma.

And it had worked. The nightmares went away. I soon made a new friend. Clara.

It had seemed like things were finally going right.

Until Vanessa took us to her house after school, the house she supposedly lived in with her aunt Tilda.

The house in the woods behind Grandma Jeannie's. The house we were never supposed to enter. But just like the no-dolls rule, this one seemed silly. Vanessa was a friend. She was kind. She would never have hurt us. And she lived there with her aunt Tilda, not Beryl.

Vanessa's aunt wasn't there.

But the dolls were.

Hundreds of them, lining the walls. Sitting in the pots and pans in the kitchen. Poking out of shoes and closets and cupboards. All shapes and sizes. All of them turned to face away from us.

That had been the beginning of the end.

The nightmares started to get worse, and the voice from the woods louder. And Grandma Jeannie was getting more and more frantic, declaring that Beryl was breaking free, that she would take us. Just as she had taken some of Josie's classmates that week. Everyone in school started getting meaner. More suspicious.

Clara had been my only friend.

When she told me I should run away with her, I believed her. After all, this town clearly didn't want me. I should go somewhere that did. She said

I could come with her. Somewhere better than here. Somewhere I'd be cared for.

She led me to the woods.

I thought she was taking me on a secret path out of town.

Instead, she took me straight to the old cabin behind Grandma Jeannie's house. The cabin Vanessa had taken us to. I knew in that moment it was a trap. I tried to run away.

But it was too late. Clara had clamped on to my arm and dragged me inside, and when the door slammed and locked behind me, I was trapped.

Trapped with a monster that seemed to bleed from the shadows themselves. A woman who towered above me in the hall, her eyes blazing white and her hair as wild and snakelike as her shadowy dress. A woman who was more monster than mortal.

A woman who made even the silent dolls lining the hallway scream in terror.

Beryl.

She reached for me with her clawed, gnarled hands. Grabbed my shoulders.

But rather than kill me, she had looped a glittering

gold locket around my neck. The same one I'd seen Vanessa wearing.

It had frozen me.

Transformed me.

Leeched the color and life from my skin, turned it into porcelain. Turned my throat to glass and froze my lips closed and my eyes open so I couldn't scream, couldn't look away.

It had taken seconds, but it felt like a lifetime.

I couldn't move. Couldn't do a thing except stare out the prison of my body as Beryl hid me away in her back room.

Nothing but a doll.

Cold.

Frozen.

Lifeless.

And yet very much alive.

Just like every other doll trapped in that place.

I'd thought I was done for. Thought I would never feel human again.

And then Josie had come to my rescue. She defeated Beryl, though I never saw how. I and all the doll-children had been freed. Vanessa, it had turned out, was actually one of Beryl's former friends, named Victoria. She'd been trapped as a doll and forced to do Beryl's bidding—just as Clara had been. Victoria had returned to her true age in an instant and passed away, while Clara had disappeared.

When Josie and I went home, hand in hand, it felt like we had been bonded stronger than ever before. We promised not to tell anyone—not even Grandma Jeannie. And after that, things seemed to go back to normal.

How in the world had I forgotten all that?

Except . . .

My memory shifted sluggishly.

There had been a moment. Our last day here. Mom was readying the car, and Grandma Jeannie took Josie and me aside. She had been trembling, and she looked sad. I figured it was because she was saying good-bye. She pressed her fingers to each of our foreheads and whispered something under her breath.

This will all just be a bad dream, she'd said. I'd felt that strange spark of electricity.

After that . . . after that, our time here had been nothing but a distant nightmare, a wisp of memory.

I gasped in realization: She had enchanted us, had made it so we couldn't remember a thing.

Except I was remembering now, and that made me feel like I had started something I couldn't stop.

It made me wonder . . . was Josie remembering everything, too? Or was her memory as faded as mine had been?

Footsteps echoed down the hall, and a moment later, Josie threw open the door.

"Wake up, loser, it's time for—"

Her eyes snared on the open windows.

"What did you do?" she gasped. Immediately, she stormed into the room and slammed the windows shut.

"I—I was hot."

She turned to face me, and I was surprised to see that her eyes were red, as if she were holding back tears.

"You idiot," she whispered, and I flinched back at the anger and disapproval in her voice. "You don't have any idea what you've done. It's not safe—don't you get it? Do you *want* her to find us?"

I couldn't answer. Because my dreams still itched at the corner of my memory, and I knew precisely who she was talking about. Beryl. The witch in the woods. The witch Grandma had spent her entire life trying to protect us from. The witch who had turned me into a doll, and who Josie had defeated.

"But . . . but she's gone," I whispered.

Josie swallowed hard and stomped to the door. She put one hand on the knob, then looked back at me.

"Evil never dies," she said. "You better hope she's really gone. Otherwise . . ." She bit her lip and looked to the woods beyond the window. "Otherwise I don't know if I can save you again when she comes back."

She slammed the door shut before I could answer.

I flopped back against the headboard.

And there, leaning against the wall, once hidden behind the door Josie just slammed shut, was the doll from the cabin in her tattered black dress.

Beryl.

33

I slapped my hands over my mouth to keep myself from screaming.

The doll stood against the wall, staring at me with her wild white eyes.

For a moment, I considered calling out to Josie. But her final words echoed in my head. *I don't know if I can save you again when she comes back.*

Beryl was here. *Here!*

Or, at least, the doll of her was.

How had she gotten in? Was it truly Beryl?

I thought Josie had defeated her five years ago!

Unless . . .

Evil never dies, Josie had warned.

What if she'd only been able to trap Beryl, not kill her? What if this doll was all that was left?

I stared at her for a long while, trying to come up with a plan of attack, waiting for her to move, to scuttle toward me like a terrible spider. She didn't. She just stood there, staring back. But just like with other dolls, I swore I could hear her whispering, whispering dark words and darker thoughts. Words and thoughts that shadowed my own, took me over . . .

Succumb to me. Free me. Together, we can rule . . .

I closed my eyes and squeezed my hands over my ears, trying to force out the noise like Grandma had taught me years ago. It worked. Beryl's voice died down, and when it did, one thing was perfectly clear:

I had to get rid of it. For good.

And since it clearly didn't plan on staying put in the cabin, that meant more drastic measures.

Maybe I could trap it in a duffel bag and throw it

out with the rest of the trash? Yeah, that would get it far, far away from here, before it could do any more damage.

Except, when I opened my eyes, the doll

was

gone.

34

I searched everywhere.

Under my bed.

In my closet.

I tossed aside piles of clothes and ripped through moving boxes, so loudly I fully expected Josie or Mom to come in.

I wished they'd come in.

The doll wasn't anywhere.

As if she'd never been here.

As if it had all been a part of my imagination.

But even though I couldn't see her, I knew she was still in the house. In my room.

I could feel her watching in the shadows.
Waiting for me to turn my back.
Waiting for my guard to drop.
   Waiting to attack.

35

An hour passed before I made my way downstairs, and only then because Mom knocked on my door and said we needed to get started. She looked around my now-messy room with concern clear on her face. But she didn't say anything.

I really wished she would say something. I was ready to burst.

Beryl had been in my room. Beryl was *here*. We were in *danger*.

And yet . . . without proof, Mom would think I was acting out. Would believe me even less than she did her own mother. The only person who would believe me was Josie, but I knew I could never admit to her there was a doll in the house.

She would freak out.

Especially because I knew she would ask how it got here. And if I told her I went into the house in the woods, breaking yet *another* of Grandma's rules, she'd be more vicious than Beryl.

I had to deal with this on my own.

While Mom and I continued moving from room to room, sorting out belongings and listening to the scratchy radio, I felt Beryl's presence. Waiting behind every book, every stack of boxes, every pile of old clothes. Always just out of sight. Taunting me. Tormenting me. As the day wore on, I still couldn't figure out how to stop her—I had never asked Josie what she did. Maybe I should have. Now it was too late, and my frustration and fear made tears well in the corners of my eyes.

"Are you okay, honey?" Mom asked.

"Just the dust," I lied.

The truth was, there was no one around who could help me. Or, at least, *would* help me. Once more, Grandma Jeannie's absence was a stab to the heart.

She was the only one who could have helped without judging. The only one who would have known how to keep us safe.

Maybe there's something else in the book? I thought.

Maybe if I could sneak away, I'd be able to find some charm or spell to get rid of the doll and keep everyone safe and make all of this just a bad dream. The thought was the first ray of hope I'd felt all morning, though it was quickly dashed.

How could I get there without rousing the suspicion of Mom or Josie?

I'd find a way. I had to.

At least, so long as Mom was in the room, it felt safer. I knew Beryl wouldn't show herself with an adult around.

With new resolve, I yanked another chunk of books down from the bookshelf and yelped in surprise.

The doll sat on the shelf, arms upraised and taloned fingers reaching straight for me.

36

"What is it?" Mom asked.

I quickly shoved the books back on the shelf. My heart hammered so loud in my eardrums I could barely hear Mom's alarmed question. All I knew was, I couldn't let her see the doll.

It wasn't safe.

"A spider!" I said, the lie quickly coming to my tongue. "A big hairy one, too."

"Ewww," Mom replied. She hated spiders almost as much as I did. "Did you squish it?"

"I don't know," I replied. "I think it got away." *I can't let the doll get away!*

"Gross," she said. "I'm gonna go run and grab the spray, just in case it comes back."

She stood from the pile of clothes she'd been organizing and headed toward the kitchen.

Quickly, before she returned, I grabbed one of Grandma's old scarves. I figured I could wrap the doll in the scarf and run it to the bins outside. Maybe try to find a way to lock it in the trash so it couldn't escape.

I pulled out the books again, hands trembling like I was unearthing a monster.

The doll wasn't there.

37

I scoured the room until Mom got back, peeking behind books and tossing aside clothes, but I couldn't find the doll. She wasn't just hiding. Wasn't just waiting for the perfect time to attack.

She was tormenting me.

I couldn't focus. Everywhere I turned, I expected to see the doll. Expected Josie or Mom to yell out at any moment, terrified or furious to find the doll waiting for them in the shadows. Knowing that she was trying to make my life miserable was almost worse than thinking she was planning on attacking. Because who knew how long this would go on?

After a few more hours of sorting, Mom declared that she was going to bring some stuff to the donation site. She asked if I wanted to come with. A part of me wanted to. Wanted to get as far away from this house and the stalking doll as I could.

The rest knew that I had brought this mess into the house, and that meant it was up to me to fix it. This would be my chance to check out Grandma's book without anyone watching. The doll of Beryl was alive, and I needed a way to get it out of the house and out of my life before something bad happened. Like Josie discovering her. Or worse.

"I'll get started on dinner," I said as Mom got ready with Josie. It was only late afternoon, but it would be evening by the time they got back.

"Good thinking," she said. "I think there's still some spaghetti in the cupboard."

"Spaghetti it is!" I said, forcing my voice to seem cheery. In truth, I couldn't stop glancing around at the boxes and bags they were carting out. I fully expected to see a tiny clawed hand, waving at me.

Mom must have noticed that I was fibbing, though,

because she stepped over and wrapped me in a huge hug.

"I know it's hard for you," she said. "Losing your grandmother. Going through all her old things. It's rough on Josie, too, but I think it's different for her. You and Grandma always had a special bond, and Josie wished she had that. I just want you to know that Grandma loved you very much. Just like I do."

I squeezed her tight and closed my eyes, inhaling the scent of her perfume. Our whole apartment smelled like her perfume—lavender and something earthy. She smelled like home.

"I love you, too, Mom," I said. Then she stepped back and smiled down at me, tears in her eyes, before turning around and heading toward the front door with a garbage bag of old clothes in hand.

I followed behind her. I wanted to make sure that she and Josie were truly gone before sneaking back into Grandma Jeannie's secret room. Josie was already out by the truck. She glared at me as she leaned against it. I knew that look. She was warning me not to break any more rules.

Little did she know I'd already broken all of them.

Mom walked out to the truck, and I was just about to turn away and head to Grandma Jeannie's room when I saw it.

Josie's eyes widened. All the color drained from her face, and her jaw dropped.

She wasn't looking at me. She was looking up. To the upstairs bedroom.

To *her* bedroom.

I knew in a heartbeat what it was she saw, what would make her look so terribly afraid. But then I heard it.

The cackle.

The terrible, terrifying laughter of Beryl, coming from the floor right above me. My heart stopped.

Josie had seen the doll.

Panic raced through my veins. There was no hiding it anymore. I had to figure out what to do. I had to—

The window above me slammed, and just as I heard a clatter of tiny porcelain feet on the floorboards above me, Josie launched herself from the side of the truck, rushing past Mom with a yelled "Go without me!"

Josie shoved open the front door.

Her wild eyes locked on me, pinning me to the wall. She grabbed my arm. Hard.

"What did you do?" she growled breathlessly.

"I—I—" I stammered, but the skitter of doll feet stopped the words in my throat.

We both stared up at the ceiling.

Josie's grip trembled on my arm. Was she scared, or angry?

Then another window opened and slammed shut. One leading to the backyard. Leading to the cabin behind Grandma Jeannie's house.

Outside, the truck engine revved to life. The noise jolted us back to reality. Josie looked to me. And in that glance, I knew she could read all of my secrets. All of my shame.

"This is all your fault," she said.

And as Mom drove away, Josie darted toward the back door, leaving me utterly alone.

38

For a moment, I felt paralyzed. Ice had replaced my legs, and my lungs were filled with tar. I could only stand there in the echoing silence of the house while Josie ran to the woods after the doll that I had let loose and Mom drove off to town.

Should I run after Mom and try to get her to help? I *knew* Josie was running into a trap. Knew she would need help.

But I also knew that Mom would never believe what was going on, and by then it would be too late.

I don't know if I can save you again, Josie had

said. She'd saved me once before. Now, I knew, it was my turn.

Before I could psych myself out, I ran toward the back door and out to the forest path.

The path felt like a living, breathing thing when I entered. The shadows seemed deeper, the air colder, the forest quieter, as if every leaf and branch was watching me. Everything was absolutely silent—not even wind through the leaves—and the only noise I heard was my feet crunching on leaves. I didn't even hear Josie. Strangest of all, with every footstep the air grew darker, and when I looked up, deep gray storm clouds roiled overhead, ominous and foretelling a coming storm. Which should have been impossible, since it was sunny back by Grandma's house. My stomach churned in fear.

What had I gotten us into?

A noise behind me made me freeze.

Josie?

But no. It sounded like scuttling. Like I was being followed.

For a few seconds, I stood there, barely daring to breathe or move, waiting to hear the sound again.

Nothing came, but that didn't ease the chills that raced down the back of my neck. I was being watched.

That, more than anything, made me push forward. I didn't want to be caught out here alone.

When the house came into view, a fresh wave of dread rolled over me.

Mist hung heavy over the yard, obscuring the broken dolls and vine-covered relics, and a light rain fell on the house, making a *taptaptap* noise on the roof. I froze by a tree, not daring to step into the yard. The house looked even more run-down now. Dangerous. Filled with broken floorboards and shards of glass and rabid animals. Shadows oozed from the open front door. I could almost convince myself that Josie wasn't here.

Almost.

Then I saw a light flash inside. It looked like a cell-phone flashlight.

Josie was in there. Because of me. Because of what I'd done.

Again.

I took a deep breath and exhaled. My breath came out in a cloud.

"This is such a bad idea," I whispered to no one. And even though it felt wrong in the very core of my being, I swallowed my fear and headed into Beryl's house.

39

The floorboards creaked traitorously beneath my feet as I made my way through the entry. I tried to walk as lightly as possible, but every single step was signaled by a groan or creak that I swore would give me away. It wasn't that I was worried about Josie knowing I was here—though I was sure she'd be upset about that—but rather . . . it was clear the house was no longer as abandoned as it had been.

Now it was practically alive.

The cobwebs seemed to breathe in the cold drafts that flickered around me like ghosts. Shadows scuttled in the corners—I didn't want to look too closely for fear of what I'd see. It no longer smelled of cookies; the house smelled of rot and dirt, like a trash bag left on a sunny sidewalk. It made my stomach gurgle nauseously. I didn't turn around, though.

Josie was in here somewhere. And if she got hurt, or in trouble, it would all be my fault.

I held my breath for a moment and waited.

Creak.

It came from a room at the far end of the hall. The room where the necklace had been kept. The room where I had been turned into a doll.

I continued on and found Josie inside.

Josie pulled down books from the shelves, muttering to herself as she did so. I had no idea what she was looking for, but it was clear she hadn't found it. Books lay strewn in piles across the floor, along with small statues and other weird knickknacks. All the drawers had been ripped open or torn to the floor.

"It has to be here," she muttered, throwing another book to the side. I'd rarely seen her this frustrated or angry before. She was tearing the room apart, and tears ran down her face.

"Josie?" I whispered.

She yelped and turned on the spot, dropping a stack of books with a loud THUD in the process.

"Where is she?" Josie asked.

The question made me freeze.

"Who?"

"Don't play stupid," she said. She took a step toward me, her whole body shaking. "I know you were out here yesterday. I know you took her. I know you broke Grandma Jeannie's rules!"

"I didn't break—"

"Don't lie to me!" she yelled. "I saw the doll in the window! Just as I saw her run back here. Why did you come here? Why? Why would you do that? Do you have any idea what she's done? What *you've* done?"

She stood there, heaving, so close I almost expected her to reach out and grab me. She didn't, though. The space between us felt charged with static electricity.

"I didn't know—" I whispered. It was the truth. I hadn't known. At least, not until this morning. Not until the doll showed up.

"You didn't know." Her words were a growl, and anger clearly overtook the fear on her face. "You didn't know what you did. Just like the last time. Just like your *sleepover*."

I froze.

Josie sneered.

"Oh, what? You think I didn't know? Alicia's older sister texted me *everything*. I know the truth, Josie. I know that it wasn't a mistake. Just like you bringing Beryl out of this house wasn't a mistake. There was a reason Grandma Jeannie always talked to you. She wasn't trying to be your friend. She was trying to stop you from being evil."

She took another step forward. So close her face was only inches from mine.

"I know what happened at that sleepover, Anna. I know what you did. Maybe I shouldn't have saved you in the first place—maybe if I hadn't, I could have prevented you from hurting anyone else. Because I know, deep down, you're no better than Beryl."

40

Ice poured through me as she said the words I'd been beginning to fear myself. I stumbled back, against the wall, as the memory of the sleepover crashed over me in a wave.

We were in my friend Alicia's finished basement. She and our other friend Soo-ji had decided on watching a horror movie. It was late and I was tired, which meant a horror movie was the last thing I wanted to watch. But I also didn't want them to think I was a baby, so I didn't say anything.

We were cuddled together on the sofa, watching

the movie, but after a few minutes, I started finding it hard to focus.

I started hearing voices. Whispers. Ones that definitely weren't coming from the screen.

I glanced around, trying to be secretive about it. And my eyes snared on a large clear storage bin in the far corner.

Inside were dozens of Alicia's dolls. Each of them with their hands pressed to the plastic, their mouths wide as they screamed for escape. The sound of their cries filled my head, drowning out the noises from the TV. I had to help them. Had to release them. Had to—

"Don't tell me you'd rather be playing with dolls," Alicia said, pausing the movie. "I thought we agreed we were too old for that now."

I jerked back around to look at her. It took all my concentration to force down the sound of the dolls' imprisoned screams.

"Of course not," I said. "I just . . . I thought I heard something."

"Mice?" Soo-ji yelped. "You don't have mice down here, do you?" She eyed the basement suspiciously.

"No," Alicia said. She looked at me and raised an eyebrow. "Are you feeling okay?"

I had tried very hard to keep all mention of dolls or voices from her, but she was my best friend. I'd definitely let slip once or twice that I could have sworn my dolls played back.

"I'm fine," I lied. It was hard to keep my voice from sounding strained. "Let's just keep watching."

Alicia nodded, but she didn't seem convinced. She resumed the movie.

After another half hour, I couldn't take it anymore. It wasn't the movie that scared me, but the yells and cries for help coming from the toy bin. Not even the screaming on the TV was enough to drown them out. Finally, I stood and faked a yawn.

"I think I'm gonna go to bed. I'm super sleepy."

"Okay," they said, not taking their eyes off the TV.

I frowned. I'd kind of hoped one of them would come up to Alicia's bedroom with me. Instead, I walked up the basement steps alone. The dolls' yells faded when I finally reached Alicia's bedroom. But they didn't go away. Not completely.

I lay down on the floor and shoved a pillow over my ear, waiting for sleep to come.

And it did come. Filled with nightmares and laughing dolls, and when I woke a little while later, I realized the laughter wasn't just coming from my dreams, but reality.

Alicia and Soo-ji stood above me, the lights in the bedroom on full glare, laughing wildly.

It took a moment to realize what they were laughing about.

When I did, I screamed.

Dolls surrounded me. Clung to my arms and legs and tangled in my hair. As if hugging me.

As if trying to strangle me.

"Did you sneak down in the middle of the night and steal them?" Alicia asked through her laughter. "You are *such* a little baby! Can't even sleep without her dollies!"

I pushed myself up to standing, the dolls falling off me lifelessly.

My fists balled up at my sides as my friends continued to laugh.

"Stop laughing," I said. "It wasn't me. You don't understand. They—"

"What, walked all the way up here on their own just so they could hug you? Please, Anna, we're not stupid."

Soo-ji collapsed into giggles, pointing.

"There's still one in her hair!" she squealed.

I yanked the doll out with a start, pulling out some hair in the process. It stung, but not as much as their laughter.

I swore the dolls were laughing, too.

"Stop it," I muttered.

The laughter swelled. And so, too, did a strange pressure inside of me, an electric tingle—the same pressure that always signaled something bad. I squeezed my eyes shut and tried to push it down. Tried to shove it deep inside along with their laughter, but I couldn't stop it. Couldn't stop them from laughing. My friends. The dolls. The power. All building. All taunting me.

All taking me over.

"Stop it!" I yelled.

My eyes flew open.

Just in time to see my friends' eyes widen in shock. Their laughs cut short.

As their fingers turned to porcelain.

Alicia screamed, and so did I, and a moment later, their fingers were back to normal, but I knew what I had done, knew what that terrible power inside me had tried to do.

I had started to turn them into dolls.

I didn't hesitate. I grabbed my things and ran from the house. I didn't stop running until a few blocks away, when I was finally able to call my mom to have her pick me up. It was late, nearly midnight, and I didn't expect her to pick up. I figured I'd have to run the entire length of the suburb to get home. Only, Mom *did* pick up.

And I received the other terrible shock of the evening.

Grandma Jeannie was dead.

41

"It wasn't my fault," I whispered, now firmly back in the present. Josie stood before me, fists clenched, her expression victorious but somehow also scared. "I didn't mean to hurt them."

"Yes, you did," Josie said. "I've always known there was something wrong with you. But that just proved it. Grandma may have thought she could save you, but I knew . . . I knew that you were like Beryl."

"No," I whispered. Soo-ji and Alicia were okay. They had turned back to normal. I hadn't hurt them. I hadn't.

"This is your fault, too," Josie said. "Grandma

Jeannie's death. She wasn't just old. She was tired. Tired of fixing your mistakes. Every time we came out here, it was because Mom couldn't handle you anymore. Couldn't stand your strangeness. So she brought you out here to have Grandma fix you. But it was draining her."

"No," I whispered. That familiar, terrible ringing filled my ears. "It's not true."

"Oh, it's true. And you know what I think?"

"Please don't . . ." The pressure mounted, screaming in my ears. I squeezed my eyes shut. The pressure in my head spiraled down to my fingertips, the power and the shame and agony as Josie confirmed everything I'd feared was true.

Grandma Jeannie didn't love me.

No one loved me.

I was a freak. Dangerous.

"I think Grandma Jeannie knew you were a lost cause. I think she was getting scared of you, too. *I think, if she was still alive, she would have trapped you out here. Along with Beryl. Two monsters, right where they were supposed to be!*"

Something within me snapped.

The pressure in me flashed out as I opened my eyes, a scream bursting from my lips.

Light flashed around me like cold lightning, striking Josie clear in the chest.

She stumbled back.

Her eyes widened in shock.

As the color leeched from her cheeks.

As her ears and nose and fingers turned to porcelain.

She took another step back. Staggered as her knees locked and became porcelain. As her body shrunk.

"You—" she gasped.

She tripped.

Fell backward onto a mound of books, landing with a quiet thud.

I took a step forward, silence ringing loudly in my ears, and stared in horror at what I'd done.

At my miniature sister, frozen on the ground.

At the doll that she'd become.

42

I stared in horror at Josie.

Her shocked face, lips parted in a gasp and eyes wide. Her tiny hands outstretched. Her skin porcelain, her eyes glassy.

Then reality kicked in, and I knelt at her side.

"Josie, Josie, I'm so sorry."

I pressed my hands to her delicate face, to the cold ceramic skin. She didn't move. Didn't register that I was there. But I knew she could see and hear me, just as I could see and hear when Beryl had turned me into a doll. She could see and hear me, but why couldn't I hear her?

Memory flashed.

When Beryl turned me, she had used a necklace. An amulet. That had been the key to her power. How had I done this without any such tool?

Was Josie right? Was I a monster just like Beryl? Or, since I had done this without a magical necklace, was I somehow worse?

I gently picked Josie up and held her to my chest, rocking her back and forth as tears spilled from my eyes and onto her soft hair. I tried to reach for that power inside me, tried to find the power that might turn her back.

"Please, please, turn back to a human," I whispered. "Turn back. Turn back."

I cried even harder as I thought of what she had said.

I was proving her right.

I was a monster.

What if I *wasn't* a good person like I thought I was? Josie was telling the truth—I'd hurt my friends out of anger, and when Josie had made me mad, I'd hurt her, too. I was dangerous. I was no better than the witch who had once lived here and tormented us.

"It's not true," I whispered to myself. "You're a good person, Anna. You're a good person."

But try as I might, I couldn't make myself believe it.

Grandma Jeannie was the only one who'd ever really believed I was a good, worthwhile person. I bet, if she was still alive, she would think I was dangerous, too. She would deal with me the same way she'd dealt with Beryl.

Just as Josie said.

I could just imagine it—living out here in the woods all on my own. I wouldn't turn people into dolls to collect them, though. I wasn't a bad person. I *wasn't* a bad person. I would just stay out here to protect everyone else from me, and Mom and Josie would go on with their lives.

But I had to bring Josie back.

Before Mom found out and realized what a monster I truly was.

If only Grandma Jeannie were here; she'd know how to help Josie. I know she would.

An idea sparked.

Grandma Jeannie was no longer here, but her knowledge was.

I pushed myself to standing with Josie cradled delicately in my arms.

"I'm going to save you," I whispered to her. "I promise."

Even then, it felt like a lie.

43

I rushed out of Beryl's house, down the overgrown path that twisted and twined with brambles that scratched and tried to tear Josie from my arms.

Ahead, the path opened.

I could see Grandma Jeannie's house through the trees, the sky above blackened with storm clouds.

I ran harder. Tears filled my eyes, and my breath burned. Something shifted on the path ahead.

A squirrel?

No. Not a squirrel.

The shape came into focus as I neared. A shape that nearly made me turn and run back the other way.

The doll of Beryl sat in the middle of the path. Blocking my way back home.

Fear turned to fury in a heartbeat. This was *her* fault. All her fault!

I grabbed the doll of Beryl in my free hand and, without even thinking, took her over to the back garden. To the patch of dead black earth waiting there.

Carefully, I set Josie aside, next to the sunflowers, and tossed Beryl in front of me, where I could keep her in sight. I almost wished she'd shatter when she hit the ground, but she didn't. Of course she didn't.

I dropped to my knees and started to dig.

The earth was muddy and cold and made my hands go numb, but I kept digging. Until I had dug a hole a foot deep. I grabbed Beryl with my muddy hands and held her above the hole.

"Stay out of my life!" I said.

I tossed her in. Above me, it started to rain.

As I shoveled dirt on top of her, I thought I saw something gold glint in the soil. But then it was gone, nothing but a mirage. Nothing but the rain and my tears playing tricks on me.

In moments, I had shoved all the dirt back on top of Beryl.

"There," I whispered. I wiped my hands on my jeans and picked up Josie. "That should hold her. For now."

Lighting flashed in the distance. Momentarily satisfied that I had locked Beryl away for a bit longer, I turned and ran inside. I just needed enough time to read Grandma Jeannie's book. Just needed time to turn Josie back. Then we could get rid of Beryl forever. Together.

Somehow.

44

I ran up to Grandma's bedroom, my feet leaving muddy prints in the hall, and it was like the secret room had been waiting for me—the bureau was already pushed to the side and the trick door was open, revealing glittering candlelight.

I stepped inside and gasped, but not from wonderment—from shock.

Because the room had been torn apart—the drying herbs had all been yanked from the ceiling and trampled, and the jars of potions smashed, their contents leaked and pooling in vibrant colors on the floor, glass glittering all over like the stars painted on the walls and ceiling.

Who . . . ?

The doll of Beryl. Of course.

But there wasn't time to worry about the destruction one doll had wrought. She was buried and out of the way for now. Josie needed me. Fast. I had to save her before Mom came home. Before Beryl dug herself free. Before this got any worse.

Grandma's book still lay on the altar against the wall, oddly untouched, as if enchanted against Beryl's attack. The moment I saw it, the cover slammed open, smacking against the trunk lid so loud it sounded like thunder. I yelped and put a hand to my mouth, trying to keep from calling out or moving, because I didn't want to step on any of the broken glass.

I watched in awe and fear as the pages of the book flipped of their own accord, shuffling with a whir until they opened to a page.

Nothing moved. I leaned Josie against the wall and took a hesitant step forward, edging around the glass. Another step, and another, until I was right over the book and staring down at what it had revealed.

There was a drawing across the open pages.

The drawing of a necklace. And beside it, a diagram of it being buried in the earth.

The necklace that had turned me into a doll. Grandma Jeannie's handwriting was bold and large at the top.

SHE MUST NEVER GET IT BACK

And at the bottom, a small note, like a journal entry.

My granddaughters and I have buried Beryl's locket in the garden, and I enchanted it against Beryl's prying eyes. So long as I live, it will remain hidden. So long as I live, it will be safe. Beryl sleeps, trapped in her house, so long as I draw breath. But if she ever wakes, she must never be allowed to find her necklace! It holds her powers, and if the two were reunited, it would spell our destruction.

My gut clenched.

A great tremor ripped through the house, sending me to my knees. I just barely missed the broken glass.

At first, I thought it was thunder, a freak storm.

Then I heard Beryl laugh.

45

Thunder shook the house, a loud roar that tossed me sideways, sending more glass jars shattering to the floor. I grabbed on to Josie just in time to keep her upright. If she broke, I would lose her forever.

Fear hammered in my chest, but not just from the thunder and tremors—I could still hear Beryl's victorious cackle.

It rang from everywhere, from the walls and the ceiling and the floor, as if it were coming from my own ears and not some outside source. It felt like she was everywhere and nowhere. It felt like she was *inside my head*!

The book before me fluttered and tossed about like a living, breathing thing. I jumped for it, slamming it closed and hugging it tight to my chest as another rumble shook me. As Beryl's voice cut through my heart.

"Come out, come out, wherever you are!"

No.

No. She couldn't be back. She couldn't be.

Fear shot through me. I pushed myself to standing and ran out of the hidden room, Josie held tight under my arm. Outside Grandma's bedroom window, the sky had grown black as night. Great thunderclouds whirled over the forest, spiraling right above Beryl's house. Lightning flashed in the darkness like burning veins.

I looked to the garden.

Or, at least, what was left of it.

A great hole had been carved out of the earth. Sunflowers lay scattered over the ground, and the place I had buried the doll of Beryl was a crater as wide as I was tall.

But Beryl was nowhere to be seen.

Movement caught my eye. And there, deep in the

woods, I saw a trail of smoke. Coming from Beryl's house.

She had gone home. She was waiting for me.

"I know what you are," Beryl's voice hissed through my ears. *"And I know what you've done. Come to me. Bring her to me. And I will set it right."*

My blood went cold.

Of course Beryl had seen. Of course she knew what I'd done. I was just like her now.

But was she telling the truth about being able to fix my sister?

I stared down at the doll of my sister, contemplating my own terrible secret. There was a chance Grandma Jeannie had hidden some knowledge in that book of hers, but I knew deep down I wouldn't find the right answers there. Grandma had never turned anyone into or back from a doll before. That was Beryl's own dark magic. Beryl's and—apparently—mine.

Beryl knew how to turn Josie back into a human.

Just looking at Josie, though . . .

What if you don't want to turn her back into a human?

I couldn't tell if the words whispering in my ear were Beryl's or mine.

The moment they spiderwebbed through my thoughts, however, I couldn't shake them loose. Instead, a new future dawned before my eyes:

I could tell Mom that Josie had just run off into the woods and gotten lost. People would look for her, and they'd never find her. If anything, they would just find the doll.

Beryl could teach me how to use whatever powers I had. Could teach me how to use them to my advantage, so when people feared me, it was because I *wanted* them to fear me.

Or maybe Beryl would, in fact, help me free Josie. My family could leave. Our lives would go back to normal. It would all be my little big secret. And Josie could never, ever be mean to me again. She'd have to do what I said. She'd have to be nice.

Or else.

My lips quirked in a smile at the thought of her being scared of me. Finally, the tables would have turned. Finally, I wouldn't be the one being bullied.

I reached down and picked her up. Looked to the quilt on Grandma's bed.

"*Anna, I'm waiting,*" Beryl whispered.

I had to decide.

Did I want to be like Beryl, or did I want to be, well, *good*?

You don't really have a choice, whispered the traitorous voice inside me. *You hurt people wherever you go. You're just like her already . . .*

My eyes glanced back to Grandma's book. Her secret room of potions and herbs and knowledge. She had been a good witch in secret all these years.

And look what good it did.

Look where it got her.

Resolved, I went to Grandma's bed and yanked off the quilt, looking out to the beckoning storm clouds in the forest beyond.

It was time to meet the monster.

46

My feet took the path on instinct. I kept the bundled figurine held close to my chest, protecting it from branches that snapped and grabbed, catching on the frayed edges of Grandma's quilt.

I couldn't believe what I was doing. It felt so, so wrong. A large screaming part of me wanted to turn around and find a different way. But it also felt like the only possible way to end this once and for all.

Despite the slow spiral of black clouds above, the air within the forest was still and cold as a graveyard, and just as silent. I could hear every breath, every snapped twig and every footfall. It felt like walking through a dream—everything hazy, everything watching. Even the shadows seemed to seep after me, following in my footsteps, knowing full well what I had done.

It seemed to take even less time to reach Beryl's cabin. One moment, I was deep in the woods. The next, I was there.

Lights glowed in the windows, candle flames flickering like winking orange eyes. The yard in front practically crawled in their light—or maybe it actually *was* crawling, the vines creeping and tiny doll arms grasping in the flickering glow. A great slow funnel of black smoke swirled up from the chimney, tendrils draping off and curling down into the yard.

A shadow passed by one window, heading toward the door, and I sunk back against the nearest tree, clutching my bundle even closer. It trembled in my grasp.

I wasn't ready to see Beryl.

Memory swarmed, a fear so real it nearly clamped down on my muscles and forced me to run away: Beryl, garbed in black and growling, as she crept closer and closer, snaring me in her spell.

How could I think I could truly confront her?

But even though I willed myself small and invisible, it wasn't enough.

The door slammed open, and out swept the monster that had haunted my nightmares.

She was even more terrifying than I remembered.

In the fade of memory, she had been inhumanly large, with talons and long ears and skin the color of old bone. But now she was all those things and more, as if five years of confinement had turned her into even more of a monster.

She towered in the doorway, her outstretched hands as gnarled as a skeleton's, each finger tipped with six-inch black talons. Her face was angular and bony, her ears stretching up through the wild mess of her black hair, her chin long and devilish, and her mouth filled with yellowed, razor-sharp teeth. The little bits of flesh I could see between the folds of her moving dress were almost purpled, her veins blue-black like a bruise. Her robes swirled around her in the breeze, half fabric, half shadow, skittering like spider legs, as if at any moment she might disappear into the darkness.

But it was her eyes that speared me to the tree.

Whereas before my nightmares had been haunted with images of burning white eyes, now those eyes were absolutely black, with shadowstuff oozing out along the edges, like whatever soul she might have possessed had become nothing more than midnight.

I shrunk back against the tree, but the moment those eyes locked on me, I felt a hook in my chest. Guiding me out into the dark, stormy yard, my feet crunching on vines and hidden doll parts, the bundle shuddering in my arms.

"My dear sweet Anna," Beryl growled. Her lips didn't move, but the words slipped between her fangs like poison. "How tall you've grown."

"You—you—" But the words caught in my throat. What could I say in front of this monster?

"I must thank you," she said. "Without your help, I might have been trapped forever."

Her hands curled in front of her neck at her words, pulling back a cover of shadow to reveal the necklace glittering menacingly.

Dread filled me, and although it was terrible to think, I felt momentarily grateful that Grandma

Jeannie wasn't here to see this. She would have been heartbroken to see what I'd done. After all her hard work to keep Beryl locked away from the world, I had come along and undone her life's work. I had buried the doll of Beryl right next to the very locket Grandma Jeannie had meant to keep from her. I had brought the monster back to life. Josie was right all along—I was dangerous. I was the reason everything had gone wrong.

And that's why I was here.

I swallowed my fear of Beryl and took a small step forward.

"I brought you back because I think you can help me," I lied.

She sneered. "Help you? How so?"

I bounced the bundle in my arms.

"Ever since I can remember, Josie has been horrible to me. I didn't think it would ever stop. Until . . ."

"Until you felt your power," Beryl finished.

I lowered my head.

Which was good, because I might have run if I had seen her come any closer—when her cold hand clamped on my shoulder, I bit my lip so hard it bled.

"I knew from the very beginning that you had the gift, Anna. That is why I had Clara bring you to me. Come. Bring your sister. There is much for me to teach you, and much for you to remember."

I gulped and nearly fell to my knees when she released her hand and stepped away. But rather than collapse, I forced my legs to stop wobbling and followed the witch into her hut.

The moment I stepped inside, the door slammed shut behind us, the loud thud punctuated with the slide of steel as the lock slid into place.

47

Beryl led me back down the empty hallway, toward the very room where I'd turned Josie into a doll, the room where I had once been held captive, too. I held the bundle closer to my chest, guilt gnawing at my insides.

This was the only way.

The only way.

Beryl's presence took up an entire corner of the room—her head just brushed the ceiling, and her wild robes still twined and twisted around her like obsidian serpents. She smiled coldly when I entered.

"Do you remember?" she whispered. "This is

where you first tasted the power." Her bony hand caressed the necklace glinting against the black layers of fabric. "The power to change things. The power to enforce your will."

I swallowed. She seemed to forget to mention that *she'd* been the one using the power on *me*. But I nodded anyway.

"Do you know why I had Clara bring you to me?" she asked, her voice raspy. "You were to be more than a simple doll, Anna. You were a *prize*."

I shook my head, and she reached out a clawed hand. Shadows swirled in her palm, becoming a heavy black orb that floated over to me. It stretched and flattened, becoming a mirror.

"Look," she said. I felt her words drip through my veins, forcing me to move against my will. "Remember."

I looked into the dark mirror, saw my terrified expression looking back. Then it shifted, and my entire world swirled away.

48

Beryl paced back and forth in the vision. She was smaller now and less menacing, though shadows still swirled around her, and her pale white eyes burned like angry moons.

Clara stood beside the pedestal in the center of the room. The necklace glinted around her neck, and her hands were clutched to her chest in fear. Her wide eyes followed Beryl's movements, as if expecting an attack at any moment. She didn't speak.

"I need the younger sister," Beryl growled. "She defies my calls. That is why I have revived you, Clara. I need you to bring her to me. Win her trust."

"Why do you need her, great one?" Clara asked.

Beryl snapped her full attention to Clara with an ominous growl. Clara flinched back immediately, knocking into the pedestal and nearly toppling it over.

"I only mean," Clara continued, "her sister is already snared in Vanessa's clutches. Once you have Josie, her grandmother will surely follow. All you need is Jeannie, and then you will be released. Why do we need the youngest?"

Beryl's eyes narrowed. It was clear she was debating between zapping Clara or telling the truth. Clara noticed as well—she quaked against the pedestal, her lip quivering.

"Because Anna has her grandmother's power," Beryl said. "Her grandmother is in no place to teach her how to use that magic. But I could. I have watched her from afar. I know what is in her heart. She will join us—she already longs to be away from her family, to be among people who understand. We must remove her sister and grandmother from the equation, and to do so, we will use Anna as bait. They will come to save her and we will trap them, show Anna how great it is to be powerful. Only then will she feel free to come into her power. Only then will she become the woman she is meant to be.

"Bring her to me, Clara. We will keep her safe. And when her family is gone, we will release her. She has the potential to become the greatest witch the world has ever seen." She cackled. "Well, second to me, of course."

"Of course, your evilness," Clara said. "I will bring her to you. And then . . . and then you'll free me?"

Beryl reached over and laced her fingers through Clara's hair, stroking the girl's head. Clara nearly collapsed from fear.

"Bring me the girl. Then, and only then, will you get your reward."

With her other hand, Beryl reached out and grabbed one of the dolls from off her shelf.

"But do not forget what comes with failure."

With a terrifying howl, Beryl's jaw dislocated and elongated, revealing rows and rows of razor-sharp teeth. She chomped down on the doll's head, breaking it clean off, then tossed the body out the window, where it landed in a heap of others. Immediately, vines crawled over the broken doll, obscuring it from view.

Beryl cackled, bits of porcelain cracking between her teeth, while Clara buckled to her knees in shock.

As the vision swirled away, I wondered who the doll had once been, and if a similar fate awaited my sister.

49

"So you see," Beryl said, her words an entrancing coo, "I never set out to harm you. I only wanted to help you. You have a gift, Anna. One that the world desperately wants you to suppress. I alone can help you embrace it."

She stepped forward, and her hand was on my cheek but her words were so entrancing I didn't have the strength to feel fear or to push her away. At the moment, I didn't want to. She was different somehow. Less a monster, and more a helper. I swear the scent of her changed into the floral perfume my grandmother once wore. Even her voice seemed to change, becoming more comforting. More . . . human.

"Think of all the times you have felt alienated or insulted," she said. "All the times the world looked at or treated you poorly because you were different."

And maybe it was her magic, or maybe the memories were just too strong to push down anymore, but all the instances flooded back.

The countless kids at school who parted when I walked past them and muttered mean words under their breath.

Alicia and Soo-ji, crying and calling me a freak, screaming at me to get away from them.

Josie, scowling when I got dolls for Christmas.

Mom, looking at me with a worried expression when I told her I heard my dolls talking at night.

Even Grandma Jeannie, and the concern on her face whenever we came over—concern that I had done something wrong again, that I needed help. Concern that I *couldn't* be helped.

Beryl was right. I'd spent my entire life being taunted or avoided because I was different, because strange things happened around me—strange things that I couldn't control.

"But what if you *could* control them?" Beryl whispered, reading my thoughts.

And then new images formed before my eyes.

Me, walking down the hall, and now kids were smiling at me, asking how I was doing, and maybe it was because they were scared of what I'd do to them—I could see the fear in their eyes, could hear the waver in their voices—but it didn't matter. They were nice to me. Going out of their way to make sure I was happy. Giving me their lunch money or fresh cookies, saving me a seat in class. Even my teachers were particularly attentive, making sure that if I got a question wrong, it didn't count against me.

Alicia and Soo-ji ran up to me after class and smothered me in a big hug, apologizing for ever being rude, saying that they loved and missed me and could I ever forgive them?

And Josie, who offered to do my homework when I got home from school and let me decide what we watched after dinner.

Mom, who bought me all the dolls I wanted.

Then Grandma Jeannie's face appeared, but rather than a look of adoration or praise, she looked at me with wild, scared eyes. Her lips parted, whispered a warning: *Anna, don't—*

Instantly, the visions faded, falling to my feet like dust.

"You see," Beryl said, "your life could be different. Better. People would learn to love you. To *fear* you. Just as they fear me. I can teach you. All I ask for is your sister. All I need is what you hold in your hands, and I will show you how to wield all the power in the darkest corners of your heart."

I looked up to Beryl. My heart raced. Could I do this? Could I truly do this?

"Tell me how," I said. "I need to know you're true to your word. Tell me how to turn someone into a doll and back again. Is it the necklace?"

Beryl stepped back. Her hands twitched at her sides in agitation.

"Very well. This shall be our barter. A spell, in exchange for your sister."

She raised her hand, and shadowstuff swirled

through her claws, much like with the mirror. Only this time, they coalesced and became a golden ring, inlaid with a jet-black stone.

"The jewelry is a spell made physical," she said, touching her other hand to the locket around her neck. "You have the power within you, that much is certain. But this is a shortcut. It allows you to turn anyone you place it upon into a doll, or back again. I will teach you how to make your own. But for now, I shall give you this. In exchange."

She held her hands out to me—one held the ring as an offering; the other demanded the figurine I clutched to my chest.

I swallowed. I looked at the ring in her hand, imagined all the terrible and wonderful things I could do with it. I knew that it was just the beginning of the powers that she could teach me how to use.

Then I looked up into the witch's cavernous black eyes, her sneering sharp teeth.

Beryl was a monster.

But so was I.

I reached out and took the ring, and dropped the quilt-wrapped figurine into her waiting grasp.

50

The moment the figurine dropped into Beryl's clawed hands, she tossed her head back into a maniacal cackle that rattled the rafters and shook the broken windows from their panes.

I didn't stick around to see.

I ran.

I didn't know if she saw me leave, or if she even cared. I just knew I had to get out of there immediately.

Dust and cobwebs rained from the trembling walls and ceiling, making me cough and splutter. Her laughter followed me down the hall and out the door, down the front yard, where the vines crawled and the broken dolls writhed, and into the forest. Above and behind me, the funnel cloud of shadow and lightning crackled with renewed ferocity, as if it was laughing with her.

My heart throbbed in my throat and tears streamed from my eyes.

I clutched the cursed ring in my sweating palm, desperately trying not to drop it as I rushed down the path and through the undergrowth that tugged and scratched.

I couldn't believe what I had done.

What are you becoming? I thought to myself.

I made it all the way to the back garden, Beryl's laughter hot on my heels, before that victorious cackle turned into a furious scream.

51

The storm broke with Beryl's scream of rage.

"ANNA!" she howled, her voice carried on the wind that whipped and howled, cutting through the trees in an explosion of branches and twigs and dirt.

I stumbled, raising an elbow to protect my eyes against the debris, and fell to the grass. I kept the ring clenched in my fist so tight that it hurt.

I had to get into the house.

Had to—

"HOW DARE YOU!" Beryl roared.

She appeared in a swirl of shadow and smoke, a

flash of lightning, and there she was, towering above the trees, two stories tall and every inch a demon. Her teeth were as long as my arms, and her eyes pulled in all light like black holes. She pointed one long, spear-like finger at my heart.

The other held the unwrapped pink horse figurine I'd given her as a ruse.

"YOU DARE INSULT ME WITH THIS TRICKERY?" she demanded.

She tossed the horse figurine to the ground, where it exploded in shadow and white sparks.

I forced myself to stand and tried to square my shoulders, tried to find some strength even though fear wanted to send me to my knees.

There were a dozen things I thought I should say—*of course I'd never join you, I'm nothing like you*—but none of them came out, because in the deepest corners of my heart, I didn't think they were true.

I didn't trick her just because I thought she was horrible.

I didn't try to get the ring to save my sister because I thought I was the hero.

I did it because I was scared.

Not scared of her.

I was scared of my power, and what I might do with it.

I cowered in the face of her fury, taking a step toward the beckoning back porch, where the wind chimes toned furiously and the screen door swung open and closed in the gale. I fully expected her to swarm toward me, to tackle me to the ground and turn me into a doll and shatter me just like she had the doll in my vision.

But she didn't move from the line of the trees.

She glared at the wind chimes and the porch and the house, and it was then I realized that a part of Grandma Jeannie's spell still held. The true Beryl couldn't leave the woods.

For now.

"You'll never have her," I said. I tried to firm my voice but failed. I held up the ring in my trembling, clenched fist. "I'm going to turn Josie back, and then she and I will figure out how to stop you. Once and for all!"

I expected her to scream in defeat.

Instead, she started to laugh, a hoarse, throaty cackle that sent goose bumps over my skin. When she threw her head back and howled victoriously, I knew that I had made a horrible mistake.

"You?" she said gleefully. "*You* think you could ever defeat *me*? You are but a bug, little one. A bug I will happily squish beneath my feet. You, and your meddling sister."

"You can't follow me," I said. "And I have your ring."

Even though they were statements, I couldn't help but feel that they sounded like questions.

"Yes," she sneered. "You have the ring. And with it, you could turn anyone you wished into a doll or back to human. But it was *my* spell, Anna. It is bound to *me*."

She reached out a hand and curled her fingers.

The ring buzzed and sparked and grew warm. I opened my fist on impulse and watched in horror as the ring . . . *dissolved*, turning into nothing more than a cloud of black smoke that swirled toward Beryl's hand, where it rematerialized into the ring.

"You know nothing of power," Beryl said. "And you never will. Bring me your sister or I—"

Just then, a new sound filled the stormy sky.

Honking.

52

I screamed in horror as Mom pulled up in the pickup, her headlights on and windshield wipers slashing back and forth in the heavy rain. I ran toward her. She couldn't be here. She couldn't—

"Mom!" I yelled out. But of course she didn't hear me. Not over the rain. Not over the wind.

Mom jumped out of the parked truck and started running toward me, her mouth open, calling out something. My name? To run?

I couldn't hear her.

All I could hear was Beryl's cackle as she raised one bony finger toward my mother.

All I could hear was the terrible rumble of thunder as a bolt of lightning speared from Beryl's hand to my mother's chest.

Light flashed.

Thunder threw me to the ground.

And when I stood up and blinked away the blur in my vision, my mother was nowhere to be seen.

53

I screamed.

I screamed and Beryl laughed and the storm clouds above us rumbled hungrily. As I ran toward where my mother had been standing, all I could think was *This can't be real, this can't be real,* even as a tiny voice inside me told me that I was too late.

Although I couldn't see Mom, the spot where she'd been was easy to find—the green grass was charred black, and heavy steam rose up from the scorch marks, the rain sizzling where it struck.

The smoke parted, and there, on the ground, was a doll. Only a foot tall, wearing the exact same clothes as my mother. Her eyes were open wide, and her mouth parted in shock, her tiny arms held before her face as if trying to shield herself from the attack. I picked her up gingerly and held her in the low light.

My vision blurred, but it wasn't from the rain. Tears filled my eyes, along with an overwhelming sense of hopelessness. *What had I done? What could I do?*

"Mom?" I whispered. "Mommy, can you hear me?"

She didn't answer. Of course she didn't answer. I couldn't even hear her thoughts. I remembered all too well how it felt to be trapped, how it felt to want to scream at the top of my lungs but unable to move a muscle.

Dolls didn't breathe. And that meant dolls couldn't scream.

"I will give you one more chance," Beryl said from the trees. "Join me. Bring me your wretched sister. And I will show you how to bring your mother back. I will show you powers beyond your wildest dreams. Just bring me your sister, or you will lose everyone you love."

Words caught in my throat.

I knew I should scream out *NEVER!* because that was what heroes did.

But I was no hero.

Instead, I considered for a moment the things that I should never have considered.

Josie didn't care about me. Not really. Only Mom did, and even that was strained. I could give Josie to Beryl. I could save Mom. I could convince her that it had been the only way—lose one daughter, or lose everything. Otherwise I would never see Mom or Josie again, and it had already been bad enough that Grandma Jeannie was gone.

Grandma Jeannie.

Just the thought brought her image to mind, and maybe it was my imagination, but I swore I could see the ghost of her on the porch, her hands on the railing and her kind eyes trained on me.

You are good, she whispered, her words forming within my mind. *Never forget that you are good and loved.*

And I remembered. I remembered the smell of Mom's perfume when she hugged me, Grandma's big pitchers of sun tea while she told me stories on the porch, and even Josie playing dress-up with me when we were younger.

I tried to push down the fear.

I clutched Mom tight to my chest.

"I'll never give in to you," I said. "I'm nothing like you. I'm already loved, and you never will be! I'll find a way to stop you, once and for all."

Beryl scowled at me for a moment.

"Very well," she said. Her scowl turned into a vicious grin. "You were right before, you know. *I* can't follow you. Not yet." She cackled low, her eyes freezing my heart. "But my *dolls* can."

She raised her arms to the sides, and out from the underbrush, covered in dirt and leaves, broken and mangled and best left forgotten, swarmed hundreds of ruined dolls.

54

I ran.

Stumbling up the back porch steps and through the swinging screen door, I slammed the door shut behind me and locked it, leaning against it and panting frantically.

What was I going to do?

Moments later, I heard the telltale spiderlike skittering of tiny hands and legs on the back porch. They scrambled over the wood and flooded against the door, hammering against it with miniature fists, vibrating it so hard I thought the wood might splinter.

I closed my eyes and hoped against hope that the door would hold.

And then, almost as quickly as it had started, it stopped.

I heard the dolls scrambling off the porch.

What were—

The windows!

They were open!

I raced toward the window over the kitchen sink just in time to see a doll that was no more than a torso and arms crawling up over the windowsill. I grabbed a saucepan from the counter and swung, knocking the doll back into the stormy yard.

But it was only the first.

There were dozens more dolls clambering to get into the window. I slammed the window shut and ran across the kitchen to shut the next. More dolls were grasping to get in, and I had to slam them away as well, the saucepan in one hand and the doll of my mother clutched under my arm. The invading dolls scattered to the grass below, some of them breaking on impact, others righting themselves and starting to scurry up again.

Even the ones that broke weren't defeated—the

remaining parts, be they hands or feet or whatever—would start crawling back the moment they had a chance. One of them was terribly familiar.

The doll in the faded sundress with the smudged smile. The doll Vanessa had given me.

She was back.

And she had brought friends.

I ran all the way around the ground floor, locking the front door and slamming shut every window I could find. The living room was filled with the terrible screeching of porcelain fingers on glass, worse than nails on a chalkboard, worse than anything I had heard in my entire life. I wanted to cover my ears and scream, but I couldn't let go of Mom and what good would that do anyway?

I looked around. The windows swarmed with dolls and doll parts, blocking out the little light from outside.

But I was safe in here. I'd closed all the windows.

And that's when I heard it.

A thud. A roll. A giggle.

Coming from above me.

Coming from my room.

Before I could question how they'd managed to crawl up to the second story, I raced upstairs, still clutching the saucepan and my mother. I skidded to a halt in front of my open door.

Dolls were pouring in from my window. Dozens. Hundreds. Swarming up over the windowsill like enormous broken ants, including the doll in her sundress. She pointed when she saw me, and the dolls charged.

I slammed the door shut with a scream.

For a moment, I just stood there, panting, hoping that Josie had followed the rules and kept the windows in her room shut. Tiny fists slammed on my closed door, demanding to be let out. I squeezed my eyes shut, tears forming at the corners.

I was trapped.

No one was coming to save me.

And then a doll clamped its tiny arms around my calf. I screamed.

55

I shrieked and kicked the doll off me, tossing the saucepan in my terror.

This doll was more intact than the rest, though half of its face was missing and its glass eye was rolled to the back of its head. It skidded across the floor before righting itself and running back at me with a silent scream.

I ran, too.

But not fast enough.

I raced down the hall to Grandma's bedroom, only to see a dozen more dolls pour out of the doorway from Mom's room, the last room before Grandma's.

I leaped over them, trying to kick them away, and raced into Grandma's room.

I tried to slam the door shut behind me, but the dolls were fast. Too fast.

They scurried in right behind me, scuttling over the floor with a clack-clack noise that sounded like angry crabs. I raced to the secret room, where I'd hidden Josie away.

The dolls followed.

I'd hoped that maybe the room was enchanted, that it would protect me from the dolls. But they passed over the threshold without any pause, forcing open the tiny door that I'd feebly tried to shut between us. The might of their pushing shoved me back, sent me reeling to the far corner. I cowered against the trunk where I'd hidden Josie. The dolls crowded within the entrance, a collection of them growing and growing, until I knew I had no hope of escape. Grandma's room was filled with the sound of grating porcelain and tapping on wood and maniacal little giggles.

But they didn't attack.

They went silent and stared at me with whatever eyes they had left, if they had eyes at all.

Maybe they were changing their minds? Maybe Beryl had gotten frustrated and called off the hunt? Or maybe they were trapping me here, waiting for Beryl to be unleashed so she could finish me off.

"Please," I whispered, as though I might have any power over them. "Please don't do this."

The dolls seemed to consider me. And one another.

A few heartbeats passed, a silence so deep I could hear every thud.

Then I heard her voice, whispered between the dolls, a rasp that hissed through my ears and tore apart my mind.

"*Get them!*" Beryl commanded.

The dolls swarmed me. Scratched me. Suffocated me.

And as they grabbed at my arms and the panic in my veins hit a crescendo, I passed out from pure, terrible fear.

56

Silence.

Darkness.

Every inch of me felt bruised, and for a long time, I thought maybe I was dead.

Then I realized I could hear rain hammering down outside, and that if I was dead, I probably wouldn't hurt all over.

I blinked and slowly saw a crack of light in front of me.

The dolls hadn't just knocked me unconscious— they'd locked me in a room.

But where?

Wincing, I pushed myself to my knees and stood upright. That tiny crack of light swayed to and fro as I wobbled. But finally, I made my way over, my feet crunching on glass as I went. I kept expecting to trip over a doll, or to have one latch around my leg or neck, but nothing else moved. Nothing else breathed.

The door opened easily—I wasn't locked in after all—and the room beyond blurred into focus.

My grandma's bedroom.

Instantly, I ran for the light and turned it on. Just enough filtered through the secret door that I could see inside the hidden room.

And what I saw inside nearly made me pass out again.

The open trunk.

The empty room.

Both Josie and Mom were gone.

57

I fell to my knees in anguish.

"No," I whispered. "No, no, no, no!"

But no matter how much I wanted to deny it, I had to face the truth: The dolls hadn't wanted me; they wanted Josie. They probably just took my mother to prove a point—Beryl had won. She would always win. She was just too strong.

I finally pushed myself back to standing and ran over to the window, hoping maybe I'd only been passed out for a few seconds and the dolls were still out there, carrying my mom and Josie away.

The backyard was empty. The funnel of storm

clouds over the forest had vanished, leaving only rain clouds in its wake.

It was almost like it had all been a bad dream.

Minus the tiny handprints on my arms from where the dolls had attacked.

Minus the scratched wooden floor and the torn-apart secret room.

The dolls had taken everything.

Everything.

Wait.

I turned from the window and went back into the secret room. Maybe . . .

Yes!

Grandma Jeannie's book was still on the trunk. A few of the pages had been ripped out and scattered to the floor, but the majority of it was intact. With a small, fleeting bubble of hope, I grabbed the book and brought it into the light of the bedroom. I flopped down on the bed and opened the book before me.

"Please, Grandma," I whispered. "I don't know how to defeat her. I need to know how to save Josie and Mom. Please help me. Please."

And just then, a breeze filtered through the room.

I looked up and around, but the windows in her room were closed and so was the door to the hall.

That's when I smelled her perfume, and felt a curious, comforting warmth at my side.

I glanced over, hoping maybe I would see her sitting at the edge of the bed, a knowing smile on her face. But of course, the room was empty. Even after everything that had happened, Grandma Jeannie was still gone.

At least, her body was.

Her spirit, I knew, was here with me.

"Grandma," I said, my voice almost a sob. "Please. They took Josie and Mom. Please help me. I don't know what to do."

Once more, the pages fluttered without a hand guiding them.

They landed on a page with very little writing on it, near the very end of the book. In Grandma's shaky, looping handwriting were the words:

I know only one thing:
She must end where she began.

Nothing else.

I flipped the page over, but there was nothing after it. All the following pages were blank.

I made an exasperated noise in the back of my throat as my tiny bubble of hope popped.

This was the last of Grandma Jeannie's knowledge, and it didn't help one bit.

58

It felt like I should gear up for some big showdown. But I had no magical potions or scrolls, no armor or sword. I only had myself and a flashlight and the words Grandma Jeannie had left for me, and the lingering hope that that would be enough.

I had to believe that *I* was enough, and after years of thinking the exact opposite, the belief was hard to hold.

Alone, I trekked out into the woods, the flashlight cutting through the gloom. Even though it was barely evening, the sky was dark and heavy, and it was getting harder and harder to see.

Every once in a while, a branch would shake, or

I'd hear the skitter of footsteps through the under-growth. Dolls. Waiting in the branches and bushes. Waiting for Beryl's command to attack. I never saw them, but I knew without a doubt that the dolls saw me. I was being followed. But that was okay, because I had no plans of running away this time. No tricks.

I was going to end Beryl and save my family, once and for all.

After what seemed like only seconds, the cottage came into view. Once more, candlelight flickered in the windows and the clouds hung ominously over-head, but now a thin trail of smoke curled up from the chimney and the unmistakable scent of chocolate chip cookies wafted over the front yard.

I stared for a long time at the front door, which was wide open, as if waiting. As if beckoning me in.

I had no idea what I was going to do when I got in there. I'd skimmed Grandma Jeannie's book, but there wasn't anything useful. She hadn't known how to stop Beryl either. Which meant I had to do what she could not. I didn't feel particularly brave or special or powerful. In fact, I felt more scared and worthless than ever.

But I had to.

It's not that I didn't have a choice—I *had* a choice. I could run away or I could face my fears. Become like Beryl or like my grandmother. Save my family, or save myself.

Squaring my shoulders, I made my way down the empty path to the front door.

The moment I was past the threshold, the door slammed shut behind me and a lock slid into place.

I swallowed.

Tried to convince myself that I had made the right choice.

Because now I no longer had any other option.

59

The very hallway seemed to breathe in excitement over my arrival. Cobwebs swayed like curtains around me, shadows scuttling with spiders in the eaves.

I knew they weren't really spiders, but dolls. I could see flashes of their porcelain skin, the glint of candlelight in their glass eyes.

Light beckoned at the end of the hall, a sliver of orange that sliced beneath a closed door. The kitchen. A shadow passed over the light, impossibly large and ominous.

I knew where Beryl was waiting.

My feet creaked on the floorboards as I made

my way, but nothing sprang out to attack me. Even the dolls waiting in the rafters stayed out of sight. I could hear them whispering, though. Could feel their words like cobwebs across my skin. They knew I was doomed. Knew I wasn't going anywhere but straight into Beryl's clutches. They were excited.

I reached out and pushed the door open.

Whereas the rest of the house was dusty and crumbling, the kitchen was immaculately clean. Candles and oil lamps flickered on every surface, reflecting off the steel pots and pans and ladles that hung from a great rack on the ceiling in the center of the room.

A great table lay below the rack, and on it rested two dolls: Mom and Josie.

I took a step forward, but the moment I moved, the shadow along the side wall shifted. Turned.

Revealing Beryl, who hovered menacingly beside an open oven. Even from here, I could feel its heat.

"Ah," Beryl said, her lips splitting wide, "just in time for dinner."

She waved her hand, and the door behind me slammed shut and locked, making me yelp in shock.

She stepped toward the kitchen table, and I took a step toward it as well. I had no doubt that my mother and Josie were on the menu, and I refused to let her harm them.

"I'm not here for dinner," I said, trying to summon what little courage I had. "I'm here to save my family."

Beryl just chuckled.

"Stupid child. Have you not realized that you stand no chance against me?" She raised her arms to the sides. Shadows and small streaks of lightning swirled around her taloned fingers. "I have powers you could only dream of. Powers that would have been yours, had you not chosen to betray me. Now you receive nothing." She sneered. Pointed one finger at my chest. "Now you will become like them."

Lightning flashed from her finger. I ducked just in time to avoid it, falling to my hands and knees. I hurried beneath the table, but it's not like I thought I could hide from her.

What am I doing? I thought. *I can't take her! She's far too powerful!*

I didn't have long to think. Seconds later, she reached under the table, her black eyes pinning me to the tile and her sharp teeth glinting in a terrifying grin.

"You're only delaying the inevitable. Come, child. It only hurts a great deal. And you've already been a doll once before. Returning will be so easy."

She grabbed my arm.

On instinct, I reached out as well.

My fingers latched onto the locket around her throat.

Instantly, my vision exploded in stars, and the room flashed from sight.

60

Sparks danced, and when they settled, I was still in the kitchen. But not the kitchen as I knew it.

Everything in here looked dated but new, from the avocado-colored fridge to the ancient oven. Pots and pans were meticulously arrayed, along with spice racks and large ceramic canisters and even a wooden bread box. Where was I? Or, rather, *when* was I?

The monstrous Beryl was nowhere to be seen, but I was far from alone.

Two girls sat on chairs at the table before me. One with lank black hair and a hunched posture, the other in a pretty blue dress and curls in her hair. Each of them had backpacks by their feet. They were both facing away from me, but I could hear them clearly.

"Are you *sure* she wasn't feeling well?" the girl in blue asked.

"Yes," grumbled the other girl. "She wanted to stay home."

"But she was feeling fine this morning."

"I said she was feeling ill!" yelled the hunched girl. "Now did you want to play together or not?"

"You're always so grouchy," said the blue girl. "But yes, I want to play. Let's play house! My parents just got me a new doll."

And she reached down into the backpack at her feet to pull out a fancy porcelain doll. It had a beautiful polka-dot dress and curly blond hair and bright blue eyes that opened and closed, which she demonstrated to her grumpy friend.

"See? Isn't she adorable? Daddy said that he had to go to three different stores to find her. I heard Victoria got one just like her."

I could tell from the way the hunched girl sat that she wasn't happy about the new doll.

"Where's your doll?" the girl in blue continued. "You know, the old one with the torn dress? Maybe we can play Fairy Tales—my doll can be the lost girl in the woods, and yours can be a wicked witch."

"No," said the hunched girl. She reached down to the bag at her own side. "I have a new doll as well. Would you like to see her?"

The girl in blue nodded vigorously.

"Oh, that's wonderful! Did your mother buy you a new one?"

The angry girl leaned over to her bag, and I caught a glimpse of her face, and the wicked smile slashed across it. That smile looked familiar.

"Not exactly," she said. And she pulled a doll from her backpack and set it on the table.

The girl in blue gasped.

"Why, that looks almost exactly like her." She looked at her friend. Her expression turned to one of fear and disbelief. "No. That isn't—it can't be."

The angry girl started to laugh, a cackle that didn't seem to fit her young body at all.

The girl in blue stood and pushed her chair backward. She dropped her doll in her haste, and it toppled to the floor and shattered. Neither of them seemed to notice or care.

"Beryl, you didn't," said the girl in blue.

She turned enough that I could see her face. A face I'd seen in countless faded photographs the last few days.

Grandma Jeannie.

"Beryl, that's Victoria!" Grandma Jeannie yelled, while Beryl just laughed and laughed. "Beryl, what have you done? You're cruel. You're a monster!"

Grandma Jeannie ran from the room, tears in her eyes, while at the kitchen table, Beryl picked up the doll of Victoria and held it in front of her cruel eyes.

"Oh, Victoria," she said. "We are about to have a *lot* of fun. At least, *I* am."

61

Beryl growled and tossed me to the side, and the kitchen exploded back into focus as pain shot up my hip.

"Stop that!" she yelled. "What do you think you're doing?"

I looked at my hands. Sparks danced over them, comforting and warm. I knew then that I had seen a vision of the past.

A vision of how Beryl's evil had begun.

And it had begun here, in this very kitchen.

I pushed myself to standing, leaning heavily against the table that held my mom and Josie. Just seeing them filled me with a new resolve.

"I know what you are," I said. "You're not a witch. You're just a scared little girl who got her feelings hurt."

Beryl growled. She expanded in size, the top of her head pressing against the ceiling and her wild hair and tattered dress billowing out.

"You know nothing about me," she said.

"I know everything about you," I replied. A strange buzzing seemed to fill my head as I spoke, along with a pressure that vibrated in my fingertips. "You said that I was like you. And I bet you're right. I bet you were made fun of as well. I bet sometimes it felt like everyone was against you, or had it easier than you. You were made to think that everything was your fault."

She didn't say anything, which made me think I was correct.

"And that meant you thought it was okay to lash out. To hurt your friends. To hurt the very people who cared about you."

I took a step forward, power filling me, and the lights around my fingers danced wildly.

Beryl—to my distant surprise—took a step back.

"You were different. Just like I am. But that's where we stop being the same, Beryl. Because I would never, *ever* intentionally hurt the people who love me. I would never become a monster like you. Because at the end of the day, no matter how monstrous you are, no matter how powerful you think you've become, you're still a hurt little girl, and until you face yourself and what you've done, you'll never have real power."

Beryl roared in anger.

"I'll show *you* real power!" she howled.

She pointed at me, and lightning flashed from her talons. I dodged just in time, but the moment I was upright, she cast another spell. This one flew by my face, singeing my hair and filling my nostrils with the tang of electricity.

Beryl cackled loudly as she sent curse after curse at me.

Every time, I was just barely fast enough.

Every time, I nearly became a doll.

I pulled deep into the power within me, felt it spark in my hands. But when I tried to direct it to her—a spark of light that was barely visible in the kitchen glare—she swatted it aside with a vicious laugh.

"Is that the best you can do?" she asked. "So much power, and you're still too scared to use it! I'm just warming up, girl. Let me show you how it's done."

She laughed menacingly and held her hands in front of her. Shadows swirled between her palms, bleeding all light from the room. I cowered back against the wall and looked around. The only thing in reach was the fridge, but what good could that do?

With a howl, Beryl hurled the ball of shadows at me. I couldn't run fast enough.

Without thinking, I grabbed the fridge door and yanked it open, shielding myself with it.

Pain shot through my left foot. I cried out.

I couldn't move my toes.

And even though I couldn't see it through my shoe, I knew she had turned my foot to porcelain.

62

Beryl howled again, but whether from success at turning my foot into a doll or anger that it wasn't all of me, I couldn't tell. Light flickered and the electric tang filled the air as she charged up for a second attack.

"Try to run now!" she cackled gleefully. "You won't get far on that foot!"

She was right.

There was no running from her. I couldn't hide behind the fridge forever. She knew she had me cornered. It was only a matter of time before she wrenched the door away and finished my conversion.

There was no way my magic was strong enough to overtake her—at least, not when she was expecting it. If she won, I would be stuck forever. Unable to scream or move. But able to see everything. I looked over to the dolls of my mom and sister. They stared at me, their eyes begging. Tears welled in my eyes. They would watch me fail.

And then I would have to watch Beryl eat them.

Unless . . .

As Beryl's spell built, I knew I had no other choice.

I had been sentient when she turned me into a doll before. I could think. Which meant maybe I could trick her.

"I hope this works," I whispered.

I let go of the fridge door. Took a deep breath. And reached for the power deep within me, the one I'd tried so hard to keep away.

"You can't hide behind there forever, little girl," Beryl said. Her voice neared as she prowled closer. "It's time to finish my work!"

Power flooded through me. Into me. It might not be enough to harm a monster like Beryl, but I was no monster. I was just a little girl. Just like Beryl said.

And I wasn't about to become Beryl's doll.
I felt the change. Felt my skin freeze and harden.
Beryl yanked aside the fridge door.
Just in time to see my change complete.
Just in time to see me turn myself into a doll.

63

Beryl's laughter filled the room and split my ears.

I could only watch, frozen, a doll by my own making, as she danced in front of me, shadows and lightning crackling around her body in her glee.

My thoughts raced.

Had I made the right choice?

Could this really work?

When her back was turned, I flexed the hand I'd used to cast my spell. My fingers still worked.

Relief coursed through me. A part of me was still human.

This might work.

Might.

Beryl turned back to me, and I stopped moving my fingers.

"Yes," she hissed. She leaned over and picked me up. Her clawed hands scratched my porcelain skin, but I barely felt it. "What a fine doll you make. And here I thought I had missed."

She turned, still holding me as if I weighed no more than a feather, and presented me to the dolls of my family.

"She has failed you!" she cackled happily. "Just as Jeannie failed you. Now that the girl is mine and Jeannie's spell wanes, there is nothing in the world that can stop me! I can take over the entire world!" She cackled to herself. "But first, I think it is time for my dinner."

She adjusted me in her arms. My free hand brushed her skin.

I concentrated all my might.

And forced the power into Beryl's unsuspecting body.

She dropped me immediately and howled in rage. I clattered to the floor, instantly turning my own powers back on myself.

As Beryl shrunk and turned to porcelain, my skin turned warm and human once more.

At the same time, she turned into a doll, and I back into a human. Her howls caught in her throat as shadows swirled around her and shrunk, as her throat turned to glass.

I hobbled to standing, blinking rapidly as my eyes filled with tears. On the counter, I heard Mom gasp out as she, too, turned human. But I couldn't look at her. I stared at Beryl as she shrunk, down and down, shadows and fabric swirling around her.

Until I was finally able to reach down and pick up the doll of Beryl from the floor. I held her out in front of me. Tiny. Blazing white eyes, tattered black dress. Her howls screaming in my head as she hammered within the cage of her doll-like body.

But she was never getting out. I had tricked her. Trapped her.

The monster was no more.

"Playtime. Is. Over," I growled.

Then I tossed her to the floor and turned to hug my mother.

Epilogue

The days after Beryl's defeat were like walking through a dream.

After turning Beryl into a doll, it was oddly simple to turn Josie back into a human. I guess once I really embraced the strange powers I had, it was easy to use them again. I expected Mom and Josie to be scared of me, but they'd hugged me and we all cried together, and it felt like we were truly a family again. No secrets. No lies.

I left the doll of Beryl on the kitchen floor, and we left the old house hand in hand.

Ten feet out of the front door, and a rumble had

made us turn around. But it wasn't Beryl coming back. Instead, we watched silently as the house collapsed in on itself, burying itself in a dirt pit from which nothing could escape.

"It's over," Josie whispered. "Thank you."

I'd squeezed her hand, and we went back to Grandma Jeannie's to finish our work.

Weeks later, we were back in Chicago. I'd gone back to school, and although kids still treated me like I was strange, it didn't bother me. Josie and Mom were there for me, and that's all I needed. Things were starting to go back to normal. I could leave all thoughts of magic and witches and dolls behind me, locked away in the past, where they were meant to be. I could focus on normal things, like schoolwork and sports and making new friends.

I could move forward.

I was heading home after school when I heard it. Barking.

I turned just in time to see a dog barreling out of the alley, straight toward me.

I yelped. But before I could run, before I could think of anything, I felt the power well up inside me.

I flinched back and closed my eyes, but the bite never came.

When I opened my eyes, the dog was nothing but a porcelain figurine on the ground.

My skin froze.

I'd done it without thinking.

I'd hoped I'd left all that power stuff behind me. I'd even left the book behind, certain Mom would throw it in the trash. I didn't want anything to do with this strange power. It might have helped me, but after seeing what it had done to Beryl, I knew it could do more harm than good.

I hurriedly picked up the dog and hid it in my backpack, hoping against hope that no one saw.

As I turned and raced back home, however, I caught sight of someone staring at me across the street.

A woman about my mom's age, with bright red curly hair. She smiled wickedly when she saw me.

She looked terribly familiar.

It was only a few blocks later, when she was out of sight, that I realized why I thought I knew her face.

She looked an awful lot like Clara. And she had seen me work magic.

About the Author

K. R. Alexander is the pseudonym for author Alex R. Kahler.

As K. R., he writes creepy middle grade books for brave young readers. As Alex—his actual first name— he writes fantasy novels for adults and teens. In both cases, he loves writing fiction drawn from true life experiences. (But this book can't be real . . . can it?)

Alex has traveled the world collecting strange and fascinating tales, from the misty moors of Scotland to the humid jungles of Hawaii. He is always on the move, as he believes there is much more to life than what meets the eye.

You can learn more about his travels and books, including *The Collector, The Fear Zone,* and the books in the Scare Me series, on his website cursedlibrary.com.

He looks forward to scaring you again . . . soon.

Keep reading for another chilling story from K. R. Alexander.

I manage to get through all my classes without getting a detention, even though a part of me really just wants to explode. It doesn't help that at lunch, the few friends I keep around spend the whole time talking about the rides they're excited to go on this weekend. Neither Felicia nor Sarah asks why I don't say anything. When I finally blurt out that I'm not going, and could they just shut up about it, I think they honestly look relieved that I won't be there. It definitely doesn't improve my mood, but whatever.

I don't need them.

I don't need any of them.

Friendship. Is. Weakness.

It makes me glance over to Rachel, who sits on her own at the far end of a corner table, face down in her sketchbook like usual. Years ago, *we* would be going to the adventure park together, no questions asked. We had many times before. Until she ruined everything by betraying me.

A small part of me wonders what she's writing in her journal—wonders if she's writing about *me*—but I don't think she'd do that again.

She learned the hard way what happens when she writes mean things behind my back.

I push her out of my mind. She could disappear for all I care.

I wish I could *make* her disappear.

At the end of the day we have a pop quiz in science class that I'm pretty certain I fail because I'm too angry at Sarah and Felicia to focus. By the end of lunch, they hadn't even asked *why* I wasn't going to the park. It's like they didn't even care!

Whatever. I don't care about them, either. I only

have a year left at this boring middle school, and then I can make new friends. Better friends.

No, friends just leave or hurt you in the end. I need to get to a point where I don't need anybody.

The only person I'll keep around is Rachel. So I can keep making her life miserable, and so she can do my homework for me.

But when I leave my last class to give my homework to Rachel, she isn't at her locker.

That, more than anything, makes me angry.

She knows she's supposed to wait for me.

She knows her *place*.

I slam my fist against her locker and storm off.

I don't go home.

Lately I want to spend less and less time there. My parents are always busy, and although my dad works in an office, Mom works from home. When they *are* home together, they basically yell at each other about always being too busy for quality time, whatever that means. And sometimes they turn their anger at each other toward me. I might have everyone at school—including the teachers—scared of me (last year I even managed to get a lunch lady fired by hiding thumbtacks in my lasagna and saying I'd overheard her muttering that she hated my guts). But home is a different story. The complete opposite.

They yell at me for every bad grade.

Ground me for every detention.

Take away my desserts, my TV time, my phone. Once, they even tried sending me to a counselor for anger management, until I threw a hunger strike and they caved.

And honestly, I might not even mind all that, because whatever, I get over it—but every time I do something that makes my parents say they're *ashamed* of me, they compare me to my sister.

My perfect, stupid little sister and her perfect grades and perfect attitude. A constant reminder that I'm not good enough.

Just like Rachel.

My sister, Jessica, is too much of a goody-two-shoes to do anything wrong, which means everyone always trusts and believes her; if I break a single rule at home or try to hide something I did at school, she finds out and tells Mom or Dad. And Mom is *always* on the edge of a screaming fit. Jessica knows it. She's basically the only person in the world I can't bully, because all I have to do is look at her funny and she cries to our parents and I get grounded or worse. No doubt she'd try to get me in trouble if I came home and did anything besides my homework, and right now, homework is the last thing I want to do.

All I want to do is yell at someone or punch something or run around because *this isn't fair*.

It's not fair, and about the only thing I can do about it is try to avoid going home like the plague. So I wander.

Roseboro is small and boring and I hate it. As I storm down the sidewalk, past the houses I've seen literally every day of my entire life, my anger builds. Not just because of Rachel or my parents or missing the theme park, but because I am *bored*. There's nothing to do around here. About the only fun thing is Rocky River Adventure Park, and even that's mostly for little kids and half an hour away. It's not fair. I'm going to be bored all weekend, just like I'm bored every other day.

Why couldn't we live somewhere cool, like Seattle or New York or LA? A place where things actually *happen* and there's more to do than go to the diner for milkshakes after school or stay at home and stream countless shows and movies. Somewhere with *cool* people who do *cool* things. *That's* where I belong. Among movie stars and popular kids who know that the only way to get to the top is to beat your way there.

Yeah. I'd fit in perfectly somewhere like that.

I'm so wrapped up in my head that I don't even realize I've taken the *really* long way home. Past the main streets, around all the suburbs, and out into the woods and fields that stretch out on all sides of our town, ensuring that nothing cool or urban ever makes its way here. It would have to push through too much corn.

For a split second I consider turning around. Even though it's sunny and a while until sunset, I know better than to be alone in the woods. I'm not worried about monsters or anything childish like that. I just know that sometimes creepy people prowl the forest. Or at least that's what my mom said when I'd been out playing in a park by myself after dark. Later that week, as if to emphasize her point, the news reported that a little kid had gone missing, presumably drowned in Lake Lamont.

They never caught a killer.

Not that I'm scared in the slightest. A small part of me *wants* to run into a creepy stranger. At least then I'll have someone to vent all my anger toward. Then the police would be totally okay with me beating someone up. I might even get a medal.

That would show everyone.

The path through the woods twists and turns, finally coming to a fork. One way leads back to town, the other to Lake Lamont.

I've heard so many stories about the lake, and even though I've been there many times, a part of me always wonders if the stories are true.

Kids drowning,

bodies going missing,

strange sounds or lights at night.

It's probably just rumors told by teens to scare off younger kids so they can have the lake to themselves.

Still, there's a voice inside me that whispers not to go there, a voice that sounds a lot like my mom's.

That's what does it. If *she* doesn't want me to go there, then *I* do.

I head toward the lake.

And surprise, surprise, when the lake comes into view, I realize I'm not the only one there.

Read more from

K. R. Alexander...

if you dare

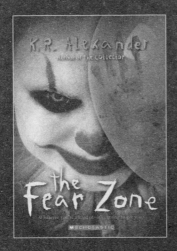

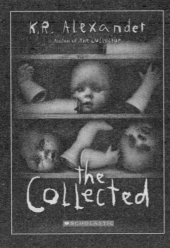

Be afraid.
Be very, very afraid...